Library of Congress Cataloging-in-Publication Data

Names: Moon, Sarah, 1982- author.

Title: Sparrow / Sarah Moon.

Description: First edition. | New York, NY : Arthur A. Levine Books, an
imprint of Scholastic Inc., 2017. | Summary: Fourteen-year-old Sparrow Cooke of
Brooklyn has always been the kind of child who prefers reading books to playing
with friends (not that she has many of those) and since fifth grade the one person
who seemed to understand her was the school librarian—so when Mrs. Wexler
was killed in an accident Sparrow's world came apart, and when she was found on
the edge of the school roof everyone assumed that it was a suicide attempt, which
Sparrow denies, but cannot find the words to explain.

Identifiers: LCCN 2017017322 | ISBN 9781338032581 (hardcover : alk. paper)

Subjects: LCSH: Suicide—Juvenile fiction. | African American girls—Juvenile
fiction. | Mothers and daughters—Juvenile fiction. | School librarians—Juvenile
fiction. | Grief—Juvenile fiction. | Psychotherapy—Juvenile fiction. | Brooklyn
(New York, N.Y.)—Juvenile fiction. | CYAC: Suicide—Fiction. | African
Americans—Fiction. | Mothers and daughters—Fiction. | Librarians—Fiction. |
Grief—Fiction. | Psychotherapy—Fiction. | Brooklyn (New York, N.Y.)—Fiction.

Classification: LCC PZ7.1.M65 Sp 2017 | DDC 813.6 [Fic]—dc23

LC record available at https://lccn.loc.gov/2017017322

10 9 8 7 6 5 4 3 2 1   17 18 19 20 21

Printed in the U.S.A   23

First edition, October 2017

Book design by Maeve Norton

Quote from "I Wish I Knew How It Would Feel To Be Free,"
written by Billy Taylor and Dick Dallas, with kind permission of
Duane Music, Inc., administered by 1630 Music Publishing Services, Inc.
New York, NY, USA, www.1630music.com

SPARROW

Sarah Moon

Arthur A. Levine Books
An Imprint of Scholastic Inc.

For Jasmine, of course.

PART 1

1

White room. White walls. White ceiling. White sheets. White gown. Clear tube dripping who knows what into my arm. Whatever it is, it's making me stupid. I feel like I've been asleep for a week. Maybe I have been. In the hall, a white doctor in a white coat is talking to Mom in a hushed, cold voice.

"Do you have any idea what might have caused the attempt, Ms. Cooke?"

"It wasn't an attempt," I croak. It barely comes out as a whisper. My mouth tastes like cotton and sandpaper. It's just as well. It's not like I could explain what I *was* attempting to do.

"No, Doctor, she's a very happy girl." The only sign that my mother is in any distress at all are the sunglasses perched on top of her head. They should be in her purse, in their black carrying case with the special cloth.

"Have you considered therapy for her?"

"No." Firm.

Ugh. I can see Mom going to the secret part of her brain where she's filed therapy, in a file she's supposed to be too

3

evolved to have: White Girl Stuff, right there with eating disorders, country music, and vegetarianism. The Cookes don't do therapy. The Cookes can handle it on their own.

"Well, I'm afraid that's the best option for Sparrow. She's past the obligatory stay for suicide watch, and she hasn't been responsive to our questions here."

Thanks for selling me out, Doc. I wasn't being unresponsive; it's just that everyone kept asking me why I'd tried to kill myself. Every time I explained that I didn't try to kill myself, the doctors, nurses, shrinks, they'd all say, "So, what were you doing on the edge of the roof?" And then I'd have nothing to say. They'd start talking about denial in their horrible, even voices like they knew they were right all along. Unresponsive.

"We can look into a longer-term facility for her, until she's cooperative, or we can recommend a therapist and release her to your care."

If it's possible, my mouth goes even drier. The Cookes don't do this. Don't need help. Don't end up in a hospital at fourteen. Please, Mom. Just take me home.

"I'll be taking her home, thank you."

"Very well. They'll set up an appointment for her at the desk with Dr. Katz. She's very good."

～

We take a taxi home, which seems very official. It's better than an ambulance, but clearly, Mom does not trust me near subway tracks. The ride isn't more than fifteen minutes, but I wake up in front of our house, my head resting easy on her shoulder, my feet curled up underneath me. It's the most comfortable I've felt in days. I don't look at her face; if there's worry on it (of course there's worry on it), I don't want to see it right now. I want to be Mom & Me; we've ridden in taxis like this since I can remember, my head, her shoulder, her arm around me. Her arm is around me now, but when she feels me stir, she takes it off.

We live in the top two floors of a brownstone, and I check to see if George, our first-floor tenant, is home. His yellow bike is usually chained to the iron gate, but it's gone—he's at work. Where my mother should be. The guilt comes in with the waking up, and through the fog inside me, I feel terrible that I've made such a mess. When the taxi stops, I get out as Mom pays. It's a strange feeling coming home from the hospital; I haven't done it since I was a baby, of course. My mom tells that story all the time. My tininess, how Aunt Joan and Grandma and Grandpa came and stayed with us off and on for weeks. They said it was to help out; Mom says it was because they just couldn't get enough of my baby smell and my baby hands and my baby self. She says she named me Sparrow because I was so small and brown, almost breakable, but so strong. Tiny but mighty, she said, that's my Sparrow.

It was just me and Mom; it always has been. Don't look for some sad tale of the father figure I'm missing or how he left when blah, blah, blah. Mom didn't want a husband; she wanted a baby. So she had one. You know. Sperm-bank style. She picked someone who was tall, skinny, and smart, like her. So, basically, I've got a double dose of my mom. I'm not one of those kids who spend a lot of time wondering about who Pop might be. Obviously, I have other things on my mind.

I look at the brownstone and it's like I'm seeing it for the first time, even though it was just the other day that I was here, that the sun was shining just like this, that I was bugging Mom for bagel money and trying to get out the door. She handed me five dollars and told me to have a good day, and she watched me walk down the stairs and go out through the gate like she has every single day since I was old enough to walk to school by myself. Now, standing here in the faint February sun, I can hear the same stupid things that we said to each other that morning, that we always say to each other. I'm standing here in a chorus of *have a good day you too love you you too do you have money for lunch yeah don't forget your homework I didn't I'm working late I know don't stay up late I won't love you you too.* It feels like years ago. It was Tuesday morning.

I could sink to the ground right here on the sidewalk. It seems easier to do that than it does to climb up these stairs that I have climbed every single day since I was a baby. I've run up these stairs crying, I've hopped up them because I was so excited to be home, I've jumped from the fourth to the first when my mom wasn't looking, I've sat out here and read for hours, spread out on the bottom two, my mom on the top two, only getting up for more tea.

6

Mom appears by my side. "Come on, honey," she says quietly. She links her arm through mine. I lean my whole weight on her to get up the stairs, like some part of me is broken, which I guess it is. When we get inside, she heads straight for the kitchen. Our kitchen is the best room in the house. The windows go all the way from the ceiling to the floor, we hung a bird feeder on the back porch, and in the mornings when I get up, I fill the feeder, make a cup of tea, and wait for them. They always come. The kitchen is white and blue, kind of like the sky. There's no table, just a big wooden island in the middle with two stools: one for me and one for her. There's a dining room with a big table for when Aunt Joan and my cousin, Curtis, come over, but the kitchen is for us. Just two stools at our island. Mom heads straight there and starts making a cup of tea. I sit on my stool, wrapping my legs around the steel ones. I remember when I couldn't get up on it by myself. She goes to the cabinet and gets my favorite mug, the green one with the black owl staring at you from the natural history museum. I got it during a field trip in second grade. I think I've used it every day since then. Other kids have ragged security blankets or a beat-up favorite teddy bear. I have my chipped owl mug from the history museum.

The red kettle starts to boil, and she pours me a cup of chamomile, pours herself a cup of English Breakfast. That's when I realize that it's morning. I look at the empty bird feeder. I want to get up and fill it, but my legs won't let me. Maybe later. Definitely later. I don't want them to think I forgot about them.

These few moments with Mom sitting next to me, her big red mug—the tea lover's equivalent of a Big Gulp—and my owl mug, steam, sun through the windows, it feels really close to normal. If it weren't for the weird blanket of fog and fatigue that's settled itself on me since the hospital—it's the drugs they gave me, I think—and the fact that I can't quite get myself to meet my mother's gaze, this would seem like a typical Sunday morning at the Cooke house. Except that I'm not in my pajamas and I've got a bracelet on my wrist from the hospital. Except that WNYC isn't playing on the radio. Except that my mom's not reading the paper; she's staring at me.

"What happened?"

I have no idea how to answer this question.

"Sparrow, honey, I just want to help. Tell me what's going on."

"Nothing's going on." This is true.

"I just picked you up from the hospital, Sparrow. How can you say that?"

"They thought I was trying to kill myself. I wasn't."

"Then what were you doing up on that roof?"

Her voice is rising, not like she's yelling, like she's scared. Like she's trying to reach me through my fog. I look at her. "Mom," I start. That's as far as I can get. Mom, let's go read on the porch. Mom, carry me upstairs and put me in bed. Mom, let's watch a *Law & Order* marathon until I fall asleep. But none of that is the answer to the question she has.

8

"Sparrow, you can tell me—it's me. I love you. I love you like I did the day I brought you home from the hospital. I love you like I did Tuesday morning. I love you. Talk to me."

I want to. I know that most girls my age have had it with their mothers. The truth is, I don't have much of anyone else. She's the person I tell things to. But there is no way to start this conversation. I look at her with wide eyes, see her eyes staring back at me full of love, full of *come on you know you can talk to me*, full of *please tell me you're okay*.

"I'm okay."

"Honey, I just picked you up from the psych ward. I love you. I trust you. But you're not okay."

"I wasn't trying to kill myself, Mom."

"Then what were you trying to do?"

This could go on for days. I break away from her gaze and stare straight through the window. I'm crying, but the tears won't come. I just have the lump in my throat, shoulders heaving. My face is completely dry. I walk through the back door onto the porch.

"Sparrow, come back, we have to talk about this."

I close the door behind me. I fill the feeder to the brim and the seeds spill out on the ground. My hands are shaking. I steady myself against the railing, looking out over the damage that February has caused the backyard. The bushes are covered in snow, dirty from George's dog, Roger. The grill is covered in snow and seems to have nothing to do with the hot dogs and hamburgers we made last summer. The ground is so dark and wet that it seems very unlikely there are actual flowers under there ready to burst through in just a few more weeks.

I wait. They come. A little stint, a couple of pigeons. They're all friendly enough, but it's the yellow-billed cuckoo that gets my attention. I stare right at him, and he stares back. Of course it's a cuckoo, here to rescue a crazy person. I close my eyes and think *takemewithyoutakemewithyoutakemewithyou*. Then I'm gone.

2

Dr. Katz's office has magazines that seem like they've been collecting dust there for years. They're mostly boring: *People* (about people I don't know) and *The New Yorker* (which seems to have nothing to do with the city I've lived in my whole life). The waiting room is painted some terrible color that needs two words to describe it: off-white, burnt ivory, eggshell. The borders at the top and bottom are lilac. I don't normally notice these things, but I do today because I am staring at the upper right-hand corner, where a cobweb has gathered above the door that will swing open any minute now and reveal the mysterious Dr. Katz, who, no matter what, is better than a mental hospital. Or at least I hope she is. I am staring at this spot where the egg-ivory-off wall and the lilac trim meet the popcorn ceiling because I can feel Mom's eyes on me again. She hasn't stopped looking at me like I'm a stranger, like an alien has taken possession of her baby girl. She is looking at me waiting, waiting for me to explain it away, to go back in time, to fix it, to give her back her perfect daughter who never gave her a moment's trouble. All that in two big brown eyes that follow me around the house, constantly trying to hide the fact that they are about to drown. I want to fix it. I want it to be easy, like making her a cup of tea when she has a headache, finding her keys when she's late, doing the clasp of her favorite necklace for her before a big presentation at work. But there is no tea for this. I'm useless, and there she is with those big Help Me eyes, so alarming in a woman like my mother, all polish and smooth edges, never a hair out of place, not even now. I'm scared that if I look into her eyes, something in me will break forever and there will be no fixing it. So I stare at the ceiling. She taps her freshly manicured nails on her BlackBerry case.

"Sparrow?"

A woman comes through the door below my spot on the ceiling. I almost laugh, but I'm too nervous, and Mom would be pissed. But I was expecting an old Jewish lady, and she's anything but that. She's tall, with light brown skin and a golden afro. She has silver glasses and a sprinkle of freckles across the bridge of her nose. She's tied her hair back with a purple tie-dye scarf that matches the flowy purple pants she's wearing. There are a few necklaces under her white T-shirt and gold vest, and they clang a little as she looks into the waiting room. And then I see the high-tops. I guess the sneakers are supposed to put me at ease, make me think I can trust her because she's young at heart, or not like the other adults I know. Right. I look at Mom as quickly as I can out of the corner of my eye. She's raised her left eyebrow in surprise.

"Hi," I say. We both get up.

"Come on in," she says, and then, to Mom, "Ms. Cooke?"

"Yes," Mom says, on her way in too. She takes her eyes off me long enough to look at this stranger. Dr. Katz places herself gently between Mom and the door.

"I'm going to talk to Sparrow for about an hour, and then maybe you and I can talk for a minute."

"Of course," Mom says stiffly. She doesn't mean it. She means, *Get out of my way.* She means, *Get away from my baby.* I hear that hard line in her voice, the same one she gets around new men in the neighborhood, the one that says, *Hurt my child and I'll kill you.* That says, *Underneath this Burberry coat and silk scarf, I am ferocious.* It kills Mom that she has to hand me over to some stranger for help, that there's something wrong with me that she can't fix. It kills me to think of her worrying, even for another hour.

"I'll be fine, Mom," I say. I manage a smile. I avoid the Help Me eyes.

I follow Dr. Katz into her office and she closes the door. There are two armchairs, a little beat-up, like they've had a lot of butts plopping into them an hour at a time for years. There's a small table with a Kleenex box against the wall between the two chairs. Unless I'm allergic to therapy, which seems likely, I don't think I'll need Kleenex. I am certainly not about to cry in front of this woman.

"Have a seat, Sparrow," she says, indicating the chair facing hers. I'm disappointed; I'd rather have the one facing the window. I sit. She puts her Conversed feet up on a small stool by her seat and leans back into her chair.

"So, what brings you here today?"

"My mother."

"You didn't want to come, huh?"

"No."

"So, why did you?"

"Like I said, my mother brought me."

"Why did she bring you?"

"The doctor said she had to."

"Which doctor?"

"I don't know his name. Didn't the people from the hospital tell you?"

"I think hospitals can sometimes miss the point. I'd rather get it from the source."

I find a ceiling corner and look there.

"Why were you in the hospital, Sparrow?"

I come down from the ceiling long enough to meet her eyes. "They think I tried to kill myself."

"But you didn't?"

"No."

"Why did they think that, then?"

Answering this question is easy. I go for it. "Because I was on the ledge of the roof at school."

"What were you doing up there?"

Everyone has asked me this question, but there's something in her voice. Like maybe she doesn't think she already knows the answer. Like she's not trying to catch me. It doesn't matter, though. It's not like I'm going to tell this total stranger just because she's wearing high-tops. My eyes find the ceiling again. It's 3:07. Forty-three minutes to go. I don't say anything else for the rest of the session. Neither does she.

Well, I think, we're off to a great start.

~

I sit in the terrible waiting room and try to listen to Dr. Katz's conversation with Mom. I can't hear a thing. Which is good, I guess, but I'd certainly like to know what she's saying. In my head it sounds like

Your daughter is crazy.

You're telling me!

Does she talk to you?

No, does she talk to you?

Not a peep.

Should we lock her up?

Probably.

I'm imagining Dr. Katz calling an ambulance to come get me, teen-sized straitjacket and the works, when my mother comes back out. She doesn't look like someone who's planning to cart me off to the hospital; she doesn't look like she's hatched a plan. She looks tired. My mother is a problem solver. She's a person who fixes the things that are wrong. I don't really understand her job, but from what I can tell, whenever something goes wrong at the bank, she fixes it. I know it's driving her crazy that she can't fix me. This time, though, I don't have to avoid her eyes. She won't look at me. We take the elevator in silence, walk to the street. I head for the subway. She hails a cab. I hate this.

In the cab, quietly, she almost hisses as she says, "The doctor has told me I'm not supposed to ask you about what you talk about in your sessions." In Momspeak, this means, *What did you talk about?* There has never been a time in our lives when there was something my mother felt she didn't know about me. This isn't true, but I know it's how she feels, and so this new privacy is totally shocking to her. Maybe I should just say that she doesn't have to worry, it's not like I'm telling Dr. Katz anything either. She sounds angry but I don't have the energy to care.

"Yeah," I say, hoping that my monosyllabic answer will be enough. "I guess the same goes for you?"

"I'm not in therapy, Sparrow, I was just making sure the woman treating my daughter isn't a total idiot."

"Sorry. Is she one?"

"What do I know?"

"She's not what I expected," I say.

"Meaning she's not white."

"Yeah. I was expecting someone like Mrs. Goldstein down the street. Are you sure it's not C-A-T-S?"

Mom almost manages a laugh. "I'm sure. She's mixed, honey. Her dad is probably Jewish."

I really, really, really want to put my head on her shoulder

16

and fall asleep. I stare out the window instead. And that right there is as far as we go. That's our entire conversation. The less I talk, the more it seems like what I say is important. I'm tired of things being important, so I don't say anything.

This week is February vacation, which at the very least means that I don't have to be in school. Not that anybody would notice, but my name doesn't have to be called in every period. I don't have to have that weird feeling where you sit at home while everybody else is doing the same thing like health or algebra or whatever and you're watching the BBC series *The Life of Birds* for the sixth time. Or whatever you watch.

The only thing that's better when I'm sick is that Mom stays home, she brings me soup, she watches *The Life of Birds* with me until she gets bored, and then we switch to something we both like. When I'm really sick, she'll even read to me. I know it's for little kids, but I still like it. She'll give me her big white bathrobe, and I'll curl up on her bed, and she'll read me some classic until I fall asleep. I always fall asleep.

This is not that. I am not sick. Or not that kind of sick. It's like I'm so messed up she's afraid to be in the same room with me. There's no soup, no *Pride and Prejudice*. It's just me sitting in my room, staring out the window, ungluing my tongue from the roof of my mouth, where it gets stuck when I'm worried. Falling asleep and waking up with a start when my mother tries to creak the door open to make sure I'm, you know, not dead. "Sorry," she always says quickly as she leaves. All we've said to each other all week is different versions of sorry.

The next Monday is the same. Apparently, every Monday for the rest of my life, I'm going to sit and stare at Dr. Katz and not say anything, and then I'll just get magically cured of not trying to kill myself. Sounds like a great plan. Mom and I sit in the waiting room and find separate parts of the ceiling to stare at in silence.

"Sparrow?"

"Hi."

"Come in." Dr. Katz opens the door for me to walk past her. "See you in an hour, Ms. Cooke."

I go in, sit in my non-window-facing chair, and look at the soles of Dr. Katz's sneakers as she settles them across from me. They are purple Nikes this time, white soles with purple trim, little zigzags like dragon teeth across the bottom, even and constant, interrupted by a very old piece of gum that makes me sick to my stomach. I look at the ceiling.

"So, Sparrow, how have you been?"

"Okay. You?"

"Fine, thanks. Have you ever been in therapy before?"

"I'm fourteen."

"I'm aware."

"No, I haven't been in therapy before."

"Okay, well, here's how it works. We talk to each other. You tell me whatever you want. I never tell anybody any of the things you say."

"Right."

"Right. Unless I think you're a danger to yourself or others, in which case I'm legally obligated to say something, but I think we're out of those particular woods."

She's looking at me like I'm supposed to say something. Ceiling.

"So, Sparrow, what grade are you in?"

Ugh. What is with this question all the time, adults? Huh? Does it reveal something about who I am? No. What it does is give you the chance to say, Oh, when I was your age . . . Trust me. You weren't like me when you were my age.

"Eighth."

"Where?"

I'm waiting for the trip down memory lane, preparing myself to be regaled with tales of Dr. Katz's high school years. The best years of her life, I bet. God help me.

"School for Vision and Voice," I say. It's the hippie public school in my neighborhood. The one that got turned into an arts school when the neighborhood got taken over by yuppies (and buppies—hi, Mom) and the parents demanded better schools for their Brilliant Darlings. We value the arts and high scores on state tests, and good luck to those of you on our wait list.

"Do you like it there?"

"I don't know."

"Do you have a favorite class?"

"I like art." As a kid you're trained to answer these

19

questions. I answer automatically. Right now I can't even picture the art teacher's face. Dr. Katz is looking at me. Waiting for more. I have nothing more to say. I look back at her. She looks back at me. It seems to me we could stay like this for quite some time. We do. I break first, go up to the ceiling.

"Do you have a favorite teacher?"

"Not anymore."

"Who was your favorite teacher?"

"Mrs. Wexler. She's the librarian."

"And why isn't she your favorite anymore?

"She died."

"I'm sorry to hear that, Sparrow."

"It's okay."

"Were you close?"

"She was nice."

I have a strange feeling at the back of my throat; it's closing up. My eyes are watering. I seem very aware of my proximity to the Kleenex. I close my eyes. I want to fall asleep. I want to burst into tears. I open my eyes and go back to the ceiling. I stay there.

"Would you like to draw?" she asks.

I stay on the ceiling. Art is just what I said because you're supposed to say something, like you say "It's okay" when someone dies, even though it's obviously not, because someone is dead and they shouldn't be. I don't even have art this year.

3

I met Mrs. Wexler when I was in fifth grade. It was my first year at Vision and Voice. It was a few weeks into school, and it was raining. I've never really grasped the concept of recess. It's loud, and there's never enough equipment (not that I wanted it, but the missing balls and bases always seemed to contribute to the noise), and it was just like the playgrounds I avoided as a kid but worse because you couldn't leave and there weren't benches. I am not a double-dutch person. I am not a H-O-R-S-E person. I don't even like kickball. I like to watch, I guess, but there wasn't even a good place to do that. It was just a lot of noisy kids trapped in a cage for twenty minutes to play a game they didn't have time to play or enough of whatever they needed to play it. If you stood at the fence and put your fingers through like an escapee, you looked crazy. I knew better than to do that. But then it rained. It *rained*! They were going to send us all to the gym, but we wouldn't fit, and so some of us had to go to the library. I volunteered. The kids all rushed in, mostly girls and a smattering of Magic: The Gathering boys. The girls threw themselves around the library like they owned it, finding tables and claiming them, making sure they saved a seat for Tiffany or Kelli or whoever. They squealed and played with their iPhones, and I snuck off into the stacks. I could still hear them, it would have been impossible not to.

"Marc is the cutest. I think he really likes me."

"There is no way that is true. Justin told me that Marc likes Melissa and Melissa likes him back, so . . ."

"You are so mean sometimes."

"I'm sorry you think the truth is mean."

"I'm sorry about your face."

And on. And on. And on.

Mrs. Wexler was terrifying to everyone. She was tall and pale, with short blond hair and earrings up and down both of her ears. She was a little old for that look, which is probably what made her seem kind of scary. Like she'd had a wild youth, but also like maybe she was still a little wild. She tamed it all with the cardigan she always wore, the only hint that she was (a) an adult and (b) a librarian. A lot of teachers take the warning approach; they'll give you a chance before they really let loose. Not Mrs. Wexler. After two minutes, she roared at the giggling girls, "You want to talk, go talk in the rain. This is the library. We read in here." They blushed so hard I could hear it. They took to writing notes. I took to looking for books, trying not to grin so as not to get yelled at for smiling too loudly.

I was wandering around, looking for something new to

read, and feeling that rush of watching someone who isn't you get in trouble. She tapped me on the shoulder.

"Something I can help you with?"

"No." I'm pretty sure I sounded terrified.

"I'm Mrs. Wexler. What's your name?"

"Sparrow."

"You're in the fifth grade, right, Sparrow? You seem new."

"I am."

"So, let me show you around. You've found fiction, I see. We've got classics over here and graphic novels there. The nonfiction is on the other side, split into sections alphabetically from autobiography to zoology. Is there anything you're particularly interested in?"

"Um. No." I don't lead with the truth right away. Besides, it was still entirely possible that this woman would eat me for a midafternoon snack if my answer displeased her.

"Have you read *Harriet the Spy*?"

"Seven times."

"One day you're going to have to talk a little louder so I can hear you, but for now" — she got down on one knee — "we'll just do like this."

"Seven times."

"It's the greatest. What other books do you like?"

"*Matilda*; *The Phantom Tollbooth*; *The Westing Game*; *Roll of Thunder, Hear My Cry*."

"Ah, the classics. Okay, let's try something this century."

"Okay."

She handed me *Out of My Mind* and *Flora and Ulysses* and *Liar and Spy*. She didn't even have to look for them. It was like she had them set aside for me. Memory plays tricks. I know that's not possible, but it's how I remember it. *Whoosh,* from out of nowhere, she drops three books into my hands.

"You know," she said as she was checking them out for me, "you don't have to wait to come back until you finish them. There are a few kids who come here every day during lunch to read. You can't eat in here, but you can be excused to the library as soon as you're done with your lunch. I'll just put your name on the list, okay?"

That's when I saw them, a handful of kids scattered around the library on rugs, lying in pairs or off in a corner by themselves on a mat, piles of books beside them. It was the first time I ever wanted to join anything.

"Okay."

I came back the next day. I didn't go to lunch. I went to the bathroom, scarfed down my sandwich, and headed right for the library.

"Hi again," she said.

"Hi." I think I managed a smile. I hope I did.

"This is where we keep the lunch-bunch mats," she explained, pointing to a stack of rugs next to the checkout desk. "Find a spot and happy reading!"

"Thanks! Um, I finished these." I handed her the books she'd given me the day before.

"Wow! Big reader, huh?"

"I guess."

She dropped another one right in my hands. *The Year of the Book*. It's about a girl who prefers books to people. I knew what Mrs. Wexler was trying to hint at. The thing is, this girl already had a friend and she just needed to learn how to be better friends. If anything, I needed a book that came with a friend included, or at least a friend manual. Cute of her to try, though. Instead, I read all the books that the main character read: *My Side of the Mountain*, I reread *A Wrinkle in Time*, and then *Hush*. After *Hush*, I read every single book Jacqueline Woodson had ever written.

"What are you in the mood for today?" Mrs. Wexler asked over her dark glasses, tilting her head a little, so all her earrings jangled. She had noticed that I was now through with everything from *From the Notebooks of Melanin Sun* to *After Tupac and D Foster*. I was stumped.

"Maybe something about birds?" I figured I could test her out now.

"Ornithology! Why didn't you say so?" She practically skipped over to the section. "Here you go, as many books as you could want on the topic of avian wonder."

"Thanks!" I'd never seen that many bird books together. I started at *Audubon* and kept going. It took the rest of the year. These were reference books, she explained, you were only allowed to take one home at a time. I came every day after that. I would always beat all the other "Frequent Flyers," as Mrs. Wexler called us. The mat kids. The readers. The losers. Frequent Flyers certainly sounded nicer.

After a few weeks, she called me out.

"Sparrow." Her voice wasn't as harsh as I knew it could be, but it wasn't her grab-a-mat voice either.

"Yes?"

She knelt next to me.

"You're not eating lunch."

"I am!"

"Stuffing a sandwich into your face in the bathroom isn't lunch, Sparrow."

I couldn't say anything. I just stared at my shoes.

"That's what you've been doing, right?"

I nodded as little as I possibly could. I was worried that if I moved my head too hard, I might knock some tears loose.

"Listen, you and I both know that the cafeteria is a terrible place, but, Sparrow, so is the bathroom. I have a little office behind the checkout desk. You can eat in there before you come read, okay?"

The world's tiniest nod again.

"Good. Grab a mat."

We never talked about it again. I just started eating in her office after that. Sometimes she'd eat with me; most of the time I'd sit there and read. Sometimes she would ask me about what I was reading and didn't I get tired of all those carrots and celery sticks and didn't I want some cookies. I did. My mom's the health nut, not me. Sometimes we'd both just sit and read and eat in silence. On my birthday, she brought me a cupcake with a little bird candle on top.

In the middle of sixth grade, Mrs. Wexler pulled all the Frequent Flyers together in her little office. There were six of us. We stood wide-eyed, nervous to be around each other. We'd seen each other every day for the last year or so, of course, but part of the joy of going to the library instead of the cafeteria was not having to talk to anyone except for Mrs. Wexler, and most of the time she didn't want to talk to us anyway. It was the first time we'd ever really seen each other. Emilio with the hearing aids; Francis, who always sat with Eric to read Magic books when they took a break from playing the actual game; Buzz, whose real name was Molly and who spent all of her time in the astronomy section; and Leticia, who seemed like the most normal person on earth. I never understood what Leticia was doing being a Frequent Flyer. She *had* friends—a quality that the rest of us noticeably did not possess, except for Francis and Eric, who were more like the same person than they were like actual friends. Apparently, Leticia just liked to read.

"We're going to have a book club," Mrs. Wexler announced.

I wake up in a sweat. I close my eyes, out of breath. I just need to get back. Just let me get back. I lie down, try to convince myself that I'm still sleeping, try to get the dream to come back. I try to see the light behind my eyelids, feel the wind in my face. I try to remember what my body feels like when it's that light, what my arms feel like when their span is twice as long, when they're covered in smooth brown and white feathers, when I swoosh and dive and soar and rise and glide. When I am just one among many, keeping my spot in our V. What it feels like to be up above, beyond Park Slope, beyond Brooklyn, beyond New York, beyond, beyond, beyond. When Central Park looks like nothing but a landing pad and there's so much blue between my body and the ground. It's not working.

I get up and head over to my window. If I can't dream about flying, maybe I'll see if I can get some actual birds to stop by. See if I can't get the real deal. Even a pigeon. It's not true what they say—they're not winged rats. Their name comes from the word for *peeping chick* in Latin, and they're just the same as doves. But even they're not coming by tonight. I hear an owl. I open the window and wait for it. Owls rarely come for me. They're just not that interested in a fourteen-year-old girl with insomnia. But I can hope. At the very least, I can wait.

My mother finds me slumped in a heap by the open window in the morning, my head resting on the sill. She screams when she see me, running to me and shaking me.

"It's okay, Mom," I say unconvincingly. "I was just looking out the window." This is not going to help me with that whole see-Mom-I'm-totally-fine thing.

The lights and the noise are the first things I notice. In that way, it's not so different from being in the hospital. I walk in and feel blinded by the fluorescent lights, deafened by the slamming of lockers in unison, the shouts and high fives and *Slow down!* and *Oh shit!* and *Watch your mouth!* and the opening and closing of doors and the *I said get in a line!* Everything here moves like Times Square on a Saturday night. If I don't pay attention, I'll be trampled. I pull over into the doorway of an empty classroom just to catch my breath. First period. I just have to get to first period. Where is first period?

It's funny how when you've been out of school for a little while — just two and a half weeks — what was second nature a few weeks ago feels like a different country with strange customs and rituals. Did I really go to math on the third floor

29

every day for this whole year? It feels like I've never been there before. But I have to go. I have to be on time. I cannot, *cannot* be the person who walks in late and everyone takes a minute to look at you and then maybe they stop to think, "Huh, where's she been?" and then the teacher is like, all solemn, "Glad to have you back, Sparrow," and then you have to go and think about really killing yourself this time. My legs start walking me there without my realizing it. I guess this is what they mean by muscle memory.

Mr. Garfield is fine, but he's new—and young. He has jet-black hair that falls into his very blue eyes. Most of the girls think he's hot; the jock boys want to talk sports with him. Sometimes he can't tell whether we're just wasting time or we really do want to know his opinion about, for example, *SpongeBob*. I never mind those times, those fifteen-minute inquiries into what he was like in high school or the Yankees. I can read. I can stare out the window. He is grateful for a quiet kid who doesn't need much from him. He leaves me alone.

We're supposed to line up outside the classroom before we come in. It's supposed to be two single-file lines, but Mr. Garfield is never very good at insisting, and we take full advantage. Today, that works in my favor. I don't have to worry about what part of the line I should be in, the front begging him to announce to everyone that I've returned, the end giving him the chance to take me aside to welcome me back personally, the middle leaving me open to comments from my classmates—if they've become people who talk to me, which they probably haven't. Happily, it's a big chaotic mess, and I can just shuffle in with everyone else.

He starts class with a Do Now—or he tries to. He's got the question on the board, $8 = 5 + 2d$, but Charmaine starts with "So nice to see you, Mr. Garfield. How was your break?" He's so happy that we're being nice to him that he tells us all about his visit to Colorado to see his family, how he went skiing. He asks if anyone else went skiing. Three boys tell him all about snowboarding; a few girls draw curlicue hearts in their notebooks. Jayce throws a spitball at one of the snowboarding boys. He hates snowboarders, he says, but I think he really means that he hates people who have families who take them snowboarding. For the whole month before break, all Jayce could talk about was how his dad was going to come and take him to the mountains. I guess his dad didn't make it. Jayce probably sat at home playing video games.

Mr. Garfield says at the top of his lungs, "You GUYS! This is *not* cool. This is not how we behave in a society. A classroom is a society, you see, a community. Who can tell me what a community is?" A spitball heads toward Mr. Garfield, not at him, not a suspension-worthy offense, just a warning shot. And I roll my eyes right out the window. It's nice to see that some things don't change.

The next period is English, and I know that I won't be able to get by quite so easily. Ms. Smith notices everything. The lines outside her classroom are always straight, single-file, and silent. They're also alphabetical. There's no way that she won't notice I'm here, no way she hasn't noticed that I haven't been here. Ms. Smith isn't mean; she's just serious about school. She's young—a lot of the teachers at my school are—and she's West Indian, which the rest of them aren't—and she has dreads down to the middle of her back, and ironic horn-rimmed glasses. She waits for us at the doorway, a smile soft like it'll go away if we mess up. We know for a fact it will.

"Good morning, everyone," she says.

"Good morning," we mumble.

"Come on in; get started. Sparrow, it's good to have you back."

She doesn't leave time for anyone to look at me or say anything, she says it right as we're all coming in, and in Ms. Smith's class, you come in and start the Do Now. It says: *Journal Day! Write two paragraphs, one about the best part of your vacation, one about the worst.* I like Journal Days because there's five minutes after for anyone to read what they've written but the journals are private. Even Ms. Smith doesn't read them. She walks around the room while we're writing to make sure that we're not sleeping or using our phones, but the actual writing is totally private.

I mostly doodle today. I can't really answer this question. It seems like a long list of worsts. Worst: Being in the hospital. Worst: Being in therapy. Worse worst: Not talking to Mom. Just thinking the word *Mom* makes me want to cry; I can't imagine actually writing about her. Ms. Smith circles our six pushed-together desks. She puts one hand on my shoulder as the other places a Post-it on my page. In her perfect cursive it says, *Take your time. We missed you.* I put the note in my pocket, curling and uncurling my fingers around it for the rest of the period.

Naomi sits next to me in science. "Where've you been?" she asks. Naomi's sentences go up extra high at the end, like a squeaky toy.

"On vacation, like everyone else." I try to sound like I think she's crazy, like I can't tell what she's getting at.

"No, I mean before that." Squeak. She looks me straight in the face, like, *You know what I mean.* Like, *You can talk to me, Sparrow.* Naomi's the resident Nice Girl. She's nice to everyone. She has big brown eyes that she bats in your direction, two pigtails that go down to her waist, and pink glasses that I think are just for show. When Naomi sits down next to you, you feel like her personal community service project, like the ones she's always announcing in assembly. I can hear her now: *Hi, everyone, I just wanted to remind you that Sparrow is coming back to school, so I'd like to invite all of you who'd like to volunteer to be nice to her to meet after assembly today.* Naomi is the person who makes the five-foot card for you and has everyone sign it. She's the person who plans the secret party for the teacher's birthday and makes sure everyone brings a treat. If you get picked last for a team in gym, Naomi will always say, "I would've picked you." You have to be a terrible person to hate Naomi, but you have to be an idiot to trust her.

"I heard you were carried out of school in an ambulance. Are you okay?"

"An ambulance can't fit inside a school, so no, one didn't carry me out, and yeah, I'm fine."

She looks so hurt. I feel like I just kicked a puppy.

"Sorry, Naomi. Yeah, I'm fine."

"I'm glad!" Squeak squeak.

Mrs. Robbins starts class. Nobody likes Mrs. Robbins but she's a yeller, so nobody talks either. I've never been so glad to be in her class.

All morning all I thought about was what I was going to do during lunch. Now it's here, and I still don't know. I head down to the cafeteria with everyone else. I don't want to, but it's so much easier than drawing attention to myself by trying to go against the swarm of eighth graders headed in one direction. So I go. Down the stairs to the terrible green room that makes the noise and lights of this morning seem like a quiet walk in Prospect Park. I get food that I don't plan to eat and look around at the sea of tables and shouting kids falling into place naturally, finding friends, saving seats, knowing just where to go. Where they belong. Naomi finds me and calls "Sparrow!" across the cafeteria, which causes other tables to look up and look at me, and I swear I see Janae mouth "hospital" to Brianna, who mouths "crazy" to Rebecca, and I drop my tray and leave. Not the inconspicuous exit I was hoping for. The lunch lady tries to grab my arm, but I'm small and I'm fast. By the time Ms. Grayson looks up from Jamal and Jarrod, who are throwing food at each other as usual in the back corner, I'm gone.

There's nowhere to go without a hall pass. I duck into the first bathroom I see. I find a stall and tuck my feet up like a fugitive. Like someone is going to come and find me. I can't catch my breath. The room is spinning, and I look for a window. What would I do, crawl out? Honestly, maybe. I let the room spin, and I close my eyes and feel my body whish and whirl and pound. I wait for it to pass.

Stuffing a sandwich into your face in the bathroom isn't lunch, Sparrow. Mrs. Wexler's voice makes me sob. I want to run into her office, I want her to tilt her head so all her earrings jangle and ask me what's wrong. I might even tell her. My heart has returned to normal, the room isn't going anywhere, I'm sobbing now. My feet against the door of the stall, my head against my knees, I'm thinking of what I would say to a dead woman and wondering how I am ever going to go to class. The bell rings. I don't know how long I've been there but someone says my name.

I don't answer.

"Sparrow, it's Leticia. I know you're in here, and Mr. Rothman is going to figure it out too. You should come to class before he notices you're gone and they go looking for you."

Leticia. I can hear Mrs. Wexler saying, *Talk to her, Sparrow, she's more like you than you know.* That might have been true in sixth grade. It might even have been true a month ago. It is not true right now.

"Anyway, I hope you're okay. I miss you, you know."

My mouth opens up, but I can't say anything. When the door closes, I take in as much air as I can. It's like I was drowning and I didn't even know. I wish I could've told her that I missed her too. That I miss Mrs. Wexler. That I miss being a Frequent Flyer. That I miss being her friend. I wish I could tell her to wait. Instead, I wait until I'm sure she's long gone and there's no one else in there. I put my feet down. I walk to the sink and run the water. I put my face right in the stream. I keep my eyes open for as long as I can. They sting. I don't care. I try not to blink. It's like I'm trying to wash my tears—past, present, future—down the drain. I'm sick of this. I stay underwater for as long as I can, until I'm choking and spluttering, but at least I'm not crying anymore. I dry my face and make sure the paper towel bits aren't stuck on my skin. I sneak into class when Mr. Rothman has his back to the door. I don't think he even noticed that I was gone.

5

"Come on in, Sparrow," Dr. Katz says with a smile as she opens the door.

There's a notebook and a purple pen on the table where the Kleenex usually is. I take my seat and begin to pick at the stitching on the arms of the chair. From how frayed it is, I'd say I wasn't the first to have this idea.

We begin our dance. She asks me a few easy questions:

"No mom today?"

"Nope."

"Where is she?"

"Work."

"What's she do?"

"Something with IT at a bank."

And on until she gets to one I won't answer, and then I say nothing.

"How's your sleep been?"

That's the impossible one today. I'm tired all the time. I could fall asleep at a moment's notice, but when I lie down at night, my mind spins and spins until morning. I think about the sky and the birds and wings and wind in my face, like I used to before bed. Still, I don't sleep. I'm worried that if I say any of that, she'll think I am crazier than she already does and I'll have to take those terrible drugs they gave me at the hospital.

I shrug.

"Are you still taking the medications they gave you at the hospital?"

I nod, not wanting my voice to give away my lie. Not wanting to show I'm surprised that she seems to be able to hear my thoughts. The truth is, Mom gives them to me every morning and I make a big show of swallowing them, then tuck them under my tongue until she looks away, spit them into my hand, slide them from my hand to my pocket, and chuck them in the trash on the way to school. My pockets are disgusting, covered in spit and dust from the nearly swallowed pills, but it's better than being drugged all the time.

Dr. Katz looks at me, brown eyes over silver frames. She takes a breath. "Listen, Sparrow, here's the deal. You don't have to talk to me, but you can't lie to me. I know you haven't had a great time lately, and I know that talking hasn't gotten you very far. It's going to take a while for me to convince you that I'm not going to tell you that you're crazy if you open your mouth. Or, I guess more important, that I'm not going to tell your mom that. I'm not. Believe me, don't believe me. But let's get one thing straight. You're not taking your meds — it doesn't seem to me that you're in any danger at the moment, but that's

38

not something that you lie to me about. It's also not something you're going to lie to Dr. Woo about at your next appointment. Do we understand each other?" I nod as slightly as I can.

"It seems to me that you're pretty used to telling people the answers they want to hear. It's a clever strategy, and I'd recommend using it in a lot of parts of your life. In here, it's a waste of time. If you decide there's something you want to tell me, there's a notebook right there. Or, of course, you could speak up, but I'm not banking on that anytime soon. Me? I'm going to put on some music. It's your time. Do what you like."

I come down from the ceiling for a second only to see if she's seriously about to put on some old-lady jams. She's fiddling with an iPod dock. She has her sleeves rolled up, and I see the hint of a tattoo peeking out from under the white cotton of her button-down shirt. I go back to the ceiling, a little shocked by what she's said, by what she knows, by the iPod dock and the tattoo.

I don't recognize the song she puts on, but it's not the hippie stuff I am expecting. It's a man's voice, which surprises me for some reason. I figured if she was going to play anyone, it would be Enya or something, something soothing and therapisty. Instead, it's a gravel-voiced white guy with an electric guitar. I can't make out what he's saying at first, but the chorus is clear:

With your feet on the air and your head on the ground
Where is my mind?

How did she know? Who is this guy? And who is this old lady who likes his music? I am tempted to ask her, but I write it down instead.

Who is this?

I sit there listening to the rest of the album, eyes glued to the ceiling. Music is something you listen to with your friends, not with your therapist, but I don't have friends, and if I don't look at the tattooed woman in sneakers across from me, I can forget where I am and listen to the insistence and heart coming through the speakers. If I'm not careful, she's going to be able to see my toes tapping through my sneakers. If I'm not careful, I'm going to dance.

It takes me the rest of the session to gather the courage to write the second question.

Can we switch seats?

When I get home from therapy, I see an extra pair of shoes by the coatrack downstairs and I know Aunt Joan must be visiting. The blare of video games tells me that my cousin, Curtis, is here too. I walk by the family room and see him completely obsessed with shooting something in some gross Shoot Lots of People game he loves. I know Aunt Joan must have told him what's been up with me because he presses pause.

"Hey, cuz."

"Hi, Curtis."

"Um, how are you?" He has a concerned expression on his face that doesn't look right. He's eleven. He shouldn't be concerned with anything but how many bad guys he has yet to kill today.

"I'm fine. Can we just be normal?"

He presses play. This is normal.

"Hey," he says over the roar of machine guns, "I got you an iTunes card if you want to listen to some Taylor Swift or something. It's on your bed."

I throw a couch pillow at him, make him lose a round of artillery or something.

"Thanks, knuckle."

That'd be short for knucklehead. This is normal.

"Our moms are in the kitchen?" He doesn't hear me; he has enemies to waste.

I walk through the family room to the dining room. The table isn't set—they must not be staying for dinner. I stop at the swing door between the dining room and the kitchen. I don't mean to eavesdrop, but I haven't heard Mom's voice in normal conversation for so long I can't help it. It's muffled but it doesn't take much to figure out the topic of conversation.

"So you think she's okay?" Mom asks.

"Donna, listen, teenagers go through things. You remember how we were."

"We weren't hospitalized."

"No, but we were teenagers. We were all emotions and roller coasters and secrets and trouble."

"Maybe. I don't know about that therapist, though."

"Why?"

"She's fine, I guess. Some hippie in pajama pants and sneakers. Like, really, are you going to be able to help my child? Are you going to be able to understand my child?"

"White?"

"Mixed. Black and Jewish, I think."

"Sparrow will tell you if she doesn't think it's a fit."

"She'd have to talk to me to do that."

"She'll come back to you, sis."

"I really hope so, Joanie. I don't know what to do."

This is what I get for eavesdropping. Everything is just as bad as I thought it would be. Well, at least Aunt Joan doesn't think I'm completely nuts. Maybe she's just saying that, though, to make my mom feel better.

"THANKS FOR THE GIFT CARD, CURTIS!" I shout so they'll change the subject. Then I walk through. It's quiet in the kitchen. They're both looking at me like I'm a wild animal who's somehow worked her way out of the zoo.

"Hi, Mom. Hi, Aunt Joan."

"Hi, baby," they say in unison. Twins, jeez.

"How are you, Sparrow?" Aunt Joan asks.

"Good. How are you?" I get myself a glass of water. I keep my voice light. I try to sound like Naomi, squeak squeak. Nobody thinks she's crazy.

"I'm fine, just catching up with your mom."

"I'll let you do that, then." I head up the stairs to my room.

"Dinner's in an hour, Sparrow," calls my mom.

"I'm not that hungry."

"You have to eat."

"Okay."

I am hungry. I may be skinny and named after a bird, but I don't eat like one. What I'm not in the mood for is sitting at the island, me and Mom on our stools, not talking, not listening to music, not reading. Picking at our meal and waiting for it to be over. I'm not in the mood for any of that.

I find Curtis's card on my bed. It's a get-well card with a little bottle of pills with a smiley face on it. It says *Laughter is the best medicine*. It's so awful it makes me laugh. He scrawled his name and stuffed the gift card inside. Still, it's the first thing that's made me laugh in a while. I sit down on my bed and take out my computer. I remember enough of the lyrics from this afternoon and I google them. The Pixies. I enter the gift card and buy the album. I lie on my bed and listen to it while I stare out the window and watch the sun set on the neighborhood. A pigeon lands on the windowsill. Stay, I think. He does. I set the album to repeat.

I wake up, and my room is dark except for the shine of the streetlights and the planes and maybe the moon. My computer is closed, and there's a sandwich on a plate on my desk. *Honey, wanted to let you sleep, but thought you might be hungry. PB, B, & J. Love you, Mom.* Peanut butter, banana, and jelly. I could roll my eyes and go, *God, Mom, just because it was my favorite food when I was six doesn't mean it still is*, but the truth is, I'm hungry and I miss her. I like imagining her making me a sandwich, imagining that it will make me happy. That she can make me happy again like when I was little and all it would take would be my favorite sandwich and a trip to the library or the park. Or just her. Then I think about her crying as she makes a sandwich for her faraway, difficult daughter who doesn't talk to her. I get through half before I think I might choke on it, or on the tears I can feel starting up.

I go to my bookshelf. I know I won't be able to sleep. I look at the books we read in Frequent Flyers. *The Pushcart War, Redwall, The Hobbit, The Book Thief*—we each got to pick a book and the rest of the group had to read it. Buzz would bring snacks, astronaut ice cream most of the time. *The Hitchhiker's Guide to the Galaxy* (Buzz's choice), *The Absolutely True Diary of a Part-Time Indian* (Mrs. Wexler's), *The House on Mango Street* (Leticia's), *Something Wicked This Way Comes* (that'd be Francis and Eric), *Flygirl* (me), and *An Abundance of Katherines* (which Emilio put on the table one Friday, terrified we'd make fun of him for wanting to read a "girl" book, but we all loved it, even Francis and Eric). The last one Mrs. Wexler wanted us to read before she died was *The Perks of Being a Wallflower*. I take it down and hold it to my chest. I can't get myself to read it yet. I wanted to read with her, and with Leticia.

Leticia's popular. She's an undercover nerd. Her hair falls in perfect curls, she speaks just enough Spanish to tell people off, and on the first day of school she came in wearing jeans rolled in the exact same way as the rest of the popular girls with color-coordinated T-shirts and the same hoodie they'd all gotten at a One Direction concert. The thing about the popular girls, though, is that they don't read, and Leticia loves to read. When we started Frequent Flyers, I stayed away from her, until one day when I came in to eat lunch and Mrs. Wexler sat down next to me and said, "I see that you don't talk much to Leticia."

"You see that I don't talk much, period. Right?" I grinned at her.

"I do see that. You should talk to Leticia."

"Why?"

"Because you've got way more in common than you think."

I didn't think much about it until we read *The Book Thief*. We read the first page, and Leticia slammed the book down and said, "Oh my God, the narrator is Death! The narrator is Death! This is so COOL!" I'd never seen a non-loser so excited about a narrator before.

After that, she started putting her mat next to mine. She'd come in after lunch with her friends and find me and sit next to me and we'd read together. Sometimes she'd stop after a sad part, and I'd finish the same sad part, and we'd each pretend not to notice the other was crying. I started getting her mat for her, putting it down next to mine and waiting for her to come from lunch. Sometimes she'd bring me a graphic novel — she likes to draw — and we'd read *Persepolis* together, and *American Born Chinese*.

Last June, when John Green came and did a reading at

the Brooklyn Public Library, we went together and stood on line starting at three in the afternoon, when school got out. We couldn't stop giggling as we got closer to the table for him to sign our books (the library said he would only sign one each, so I picked *An Abundance of Katherines* to give to Emilio because he didn't want to ask his parents to let him come, and Leticia picked *The Fault in Our Stars*, which we decided we would share). When we finally got up to the table, she introduced us as Speticia and Larrow and we both laughed so hard we had tears in our eyes. Maybe you had to be there. I still think of her as Speticia, even if we haven't talked in months.

6

The next week, I see the notebook again, but this time next to the chair Dr. Katz usually sits in. She sits in what used to be my chair and holds out her hand, inviting me to take a seat. "A little bird mentioned that you'd prefer to sit here." Usually bird puns off my name are irritating, but it's like she doesn't even realize she's doing it. I sit in her matching chair, which is less frayed but just as worn. She's taken her footstool over to her side of the room. The windows are just what I'd hoped for.

"Those were the Pixies I was playing last week. They're an old punk band. Did you like them?"

"Yeah, I guess." I guess, I went home and bought the album. I guess, I've been listening to it all week. I guess, I could listen to them right now. I want more tearing guitar and mumbled words. I want to hear more noise that sounds just like how I feel.

"What did you like about them?"

I like that they sound as crazy as I feel. I like that they make me feel like I'm not crazy. I like that they seem to know just how I feel. I like that I can't understand what they're saying

47

sometimes but I still know exactly what they mean. I like that the guy sounds like he's searching. I like the wails. These are not things you say to people. I stare at the ceiling first, but then I remember: the windows. I settle in, get ready to feel myself get light, to float up and out the window, to get gone.

Dr. Katz isn't having it today. "Sparrow."

I say nothing.

"Where are you?"

"Here. Obviously." I try to bite a little at her. Get away from me. Let me get away from here. From me.

"I don't think you are. I'd like you to try to stick around for the next forty-five minutes. You don't have to talk, but you have to stay. Deal?"

Silence.

"Would you like to listen to more music?"

"If you want."

"How about if you do?"

"Okay."

"I'll put some on. Meanwhile, I want you to take a look in that notebook. Write something if it strikes your fancy."

I want to tell her that she's old, but not that old. Maybe she doesn't want to talk like a Victorian.

In the notebook, I see that she's answered my questions. In neat handwriting, a black pen, small words say *The Pixies*. Then, below my seat-change request, a second answer and a new question. *Sure. Why?*

As she fiddles with the iPod dock, I fiddle with the pen. I don't know how to answer this question in a way that won't get me committed. Again.

I write, *Because I like the windows. I like watching the birds.* That seems pretty reasonable, like something a not-crazy person might say.

"Whatever thoughts come to mind while you listen, I'd love to know them. If you can tell me them, tell me. If you can't, write them down." Every few songs, she looks over at me and says the name of the band: "The White Stripes." My foot is tapping up and down. I've lost interest in trying to keep it from going. It's too hard to sit still during the driving beat, the pulsing guitar. There's a pain in his voice that is as familiar to me as my own name. It's the pain that would be in my voice if I spoke right now. I write, *He sounds like he's in pain. It sounds like he always has been. But strong too.*

I find myself doodling and beating on the notebook with my pen. The next song starts with a guitar that my head can barely resist. But it's the scream that gets me. I look up. "Alabama Shakes," she says, smiling at my wide eyes. I love the scream, the voice deep and big as a house. And I don't want to fight anymore either. The next song is the same woman, but the pain in her voice has quadrupled. I feel it on my skin. It feels like my skin. My eyes close. My stomach tightens with the swoop of her voice, the gravel in it keeping us both tied to earth.

Before I can stop myself, I write down one word among my doodles: *Chocolate*. Before I can stop myself, there are tears all over my face.

〜

Mrs. Wexler died in October. It was a sunny morning after a rainy night, third period on a Friday. I was in Mr. Garfield's math class, doing nothing as usual. He seemed a little more awkward that day, a little nervous, maybe. At 11:10 he stopped class early and said, "You guys"—he starts almost every sentence with *you guys*—"I have some really sad news. I'd like you all to be respectful of one another's feelings and reactions and help me to create a safe space here." It's like he's the living definition of the word *dweeb*. I don't know why these girls are so crazy for him. "Our librarian, Mrs. Wexler, was hit by a car this morning on her walk to school. I am very sorry to tell you that she's passed—um, she didn't make it, you know, is deceased. We are all very sad and very sorry. The office hired some grief counselors if anyone wants to talk to them. We'll let you know about the service. Any questions?"

I got up out of my seat and slammed the door behind me. Maybe he called out after me, maybe he didn't, maybe it was just some kid asking if this meant he could keep his library books. I ran to every eighth-grade room, stopping in the doorway to scan for Leticia. I was out of breath, sobbing, the hallways had never been this empty, I felt like I was in a movie, or a bad dream. It was just me running down the hall, making terrible sounds as I tried to breathe and cry at the same time, looking for Leticia. I finally saw her in Ms. Smith's room. Her friend, a Popular Girl named Raven, saw me before she did.

"Um, Leti, it seems like that weird girl maybe wants to talk to you? Do you, like, know her?"

I have replayed this moment over and over in my head. I was standing in the hallway, holding my sides like I was going to split in two if I let go, which I think I might have. My eyes were red and fixed on hers. In my mind, she runs out of the room, slams the door, and hugs me. She is crying too. We go and get our mats; we go to the park. We spend the rest of the day crying and talking and watching the birds come and go. Instead, what happened was this:

She mouthed, "Sorry." She didn't come. She didn't hug me. She didn't cry. I stood there for longer than I should have, waiting for her to come, long enough for Ms. Smith to come to the door, but by the time she said, "Sparrow, come talk to me," I was down the hall, down the stairs, down the block. I ran to the park; it's uphill but I didn't feel it. I guess you can't get out of breath if you don't have any to begin with. I ran through the wet grass to a big open field. There wasn't anyone around, not the dog people or the moms with their babies and their coffee and their organic snack packs, not a yoga class, nobody. I fell to the ground and cried. I don't know how long I stayed there, facedown in the grass. Eventually, a great crested flycatcher came. It landed right next to me on the grass. *Come on*, it said.

I went. I went up and up and my arms were long and my body was light and all I could see was green below me. I couldn't see some sad little girl crumpled on the ground crying, I couldn't see Ms. Smith outside the school looking for me, I couldn't see the phone ringing in my house the way I knew it would after lunch when a teacher noticed that I wasn't there. I was taken into a family of flycatchers, we were in a V, traveling together. We went over the Hudson, not the gross part by the West Side Highway, but up where it gets pretty after you leave the city, diving down to the top of the cool, moving river — our highway — and then back up to where all we could see were trees and blue water, small houses and smaller cars, the occasional train. From here, people were so small I didn't even see them. I didn't think about them. Breath came easy as we soared up and swooped down.

When they dropped me off, I was faceup on the ground, the front of my shirt wet with my tears, and it was much, much later than I thought it was. I checked my phone: 2:05. I had a missed call and a text from Mom. She'd just texted at 2:02. **The school says you left. Please tell me what's going on.** I couldn't get myself to listen to her message. I texted her back. **Mrs. Wexler died. I went to the park. On my way home now.** She wrote back immediately. **I'll be right there. I love you.**

I don't know how Mom managed to beat me home. She works in Manhattan; it's like she flew or something. Ha. Or maybe I was just walking extra slow that day. Either way, when I got in, she looked at me, my shirt stained with grass and tears and dirt, my hair with little pieces of leaves stuck in it, my face snotty. And she grabbed me to her, still in her suit, put one hand on my back and one on the back of my head, and said, "Oh, baby, I'm so sorry."

I didn't cry. I didn't feel anything. I didn't say anything, and she didn't expect me to. She picked me up—I didn't know she still could—and put me in a hot bath and picked the leaves out of my hair. She sat with me, not the way she would now—like, can't leave Sparrow alone in the bathtub because she might kill herself—but just to be near me. I couldn't move. She lifted me out of the bath and put me in her big white bathrobe. She made me a cup of tea and we sat on the stools in the kitchen.

"It's okay, baby, you don't have to talk. Death takes words from us. Just know that I'm sorry and that I'm here." She knew exactly. I wonder where that Mom is now; I wonder why she can't understand me that easy now. She held my hand and we went over to the couch and we watched all of *The Life of Birds* until I fell asleep, my head on her shoulder, her arm around me.

7

I was afraid Mrs. Robbins was going to kick me out of last-period science when I woke up with a start in the middle of one of her fifteen-minute lectures about why it is of utmost importance that we memorize the periodic table, how it's about becoming disciplined adults, how we'll never get jobs if we can't manage a simple task such as this. She gives this lecture once every few days. Truth is that if I wanted to, I could probably memorize it, but telling me that my future depends on knowing the symbol for gadolinium . . . what's the periodic symbol for bullshit?

But Mrs. Robbins didn't kick me out. She didn't even notice that I was asleep. I guess it's possible that in a room of twenty-seven kids, you don't notice one asleep. It's also possible that me asleep is not that different from me awake these days. I'm hoping she also hasn't noticed that I don't have my work. That I haven't had my homework for weeks.

My eyes are closing in this warm little off-white waiting room. I'm trying to pretend to read one of the dusty old magazines, but I don't have the energy. I snap to attention as the door opens.

"Hi, Sparrow. Come on in."

Dr. Katz is wearing a long black-and-white cardigan today; it goes all the way down to her Nikes. Her silver bracelets jangle as she crosses the room. I sit myself in the new seat. This whole therapy thing has become a lot less awful since it started involving listening to music and staring out the window.

"So, how are you?" she asks, crossing her sneakers as she settles into her chair.

"Tired," I mumble, suppressing a yawn.

"Do you normally have trouble sleeping?"

"I didn't used to."

"But lately?"

"Lately I don't sleep."

"What made it easy to sleep before?"

And so we begin. I start at the top of her head—the two stray curls that resist gravity, and then my eyes go up and up and up until all I'm looking at is the lilac trim of the ceiling against the gray-blue March sky out the window. If I stay still, I can see the clouds shift shape. They don't look like anything, the way they did when I was a kid. I don't see a clown or a giraffe or a heart or even popcorn; they're just gray shifting to darker gray and then back out to edges of white where the sky seems to disappear.

"Okay, so that's off the list for today, huh?" she asks. It startles me. I think she's smiling. I think she's joking.

"What?" I say, not coming down from my corner of the sky.

"You don't want to talk about that. Whatever the answer is, you think I'll think you're crazy and pack you off to the nuthouse or something, so it's off-limits. That's okay. Can we talk about something else, or am I just going to watch you watch the sky for the next forty minutes?"

"You don't have to watch me."

"Ha. Yes, that's very true. I could sit here and meditate, I guess, beat my next level on Candy Crush. But I think I'd rather talk to you."

"Okay."

"So, new topic. Tell me about chocolate." I'd forgotten that I'd written her name in the notebook.

"She's a friend of mine."

"Chocolate is her name?"

"Yeah. I mean, I don't know. I think she probably made it up."

"How do you know her?"

"I don't anymore. I met her on the first day of kindergarten."

"She went to your school?"

"Yeah."

"Did you like that school?"

"No. I mean, I was excited when my mom told me I was going to school, because I'd seen it on TV and stuff, but I didn't understand what it was. I thought it would be like going to the library. I got there and it seemed like everyone else had gotten some set of instructions I'd never heard about. The girls were already sitting together on the rug, they were dumping out their little-kid purses and backpacks and showing their toys to each other, and the boys were chasing each other around the room, and it was the noisiest place I'd ever been. I also didn't realize that going to school meant going to school without my mom. She was the only person I was used to. It was really scary."

I am surprised because I have heard this story so many times at family occasions about how silly little Sparrow thought she was going to go to school with Mom and how she stood stock-still by the wall and closed her eyes like no one could see her if she couldn't see them. But telling it this way, not like some family joke that makes me scowl and pretend I'm not related to them, I feel like I'm right back in that minute. Not standing by the wall (I wasn't standing by the wall; they always get that part wrong) but in between the cubbies in the corner, trying to blend in with the coats and the backpacks. I wish I had a coat to hide behind now. But I keep going, like telling this story will undo all the times that my family has told it the wrong way.

"So I hid in the cubbies under the coats and backpacks and stuff, and this hand comes through, no bigger than mine, and grabs me, like there's someplace really important we have to go and it won't be the same if I don't come with her. She brought me to the circle and she sat with me. We sat there, and the teacher asked us all to go around and say our names, and when it got to me, I said 'Sparrow' in this tiny voice, and she couldn't understand me and I had to say it like six times and I hated the attention and the giggling girls who thought it was so funny that the teacher couldn't hear my voice. And then it's my new friend's turn and she just says 'Chocolate' loud and clear. I was jealous because I wanted a name like that. More than that, I wanted to pick any name I wanted and have the balls — sorry, can I say that? — to pretend it was my own. When it was time for recess, I went and hid under the coats and backpacks by the cubbies. I could hear Chocolate looking for me, though. She called my name all over the playground."

"How did that feel?"

I shoot her a look. "What a very therapisty question."

"Sorry, occupational hazard. But seriously, how did it feel to be hidden there and have her look for you?"

"Good. Like I had a friend. I'd never had one before. And at the end of the day, she asked me why I wouldn't come to recess. And I told her I didn't like it, and she asked me how I could know that if I'd never been. The next day, she was right there at the door when I walked in, she grabbed my hand, she steered me through the chasing boys, and we sat down on the rug again. We ate lunch together. I remember I gave her half my sandwich and she looked at me with these big eyes like she couldn't believe I would be so nice to her when she'd basically saved me from kindergarten hell. It was just peanut butter and jelly; she acted like I'd given her an organ."

"Maybe she didn't have a lot of people who were as kind to her as you were."

"I wasn't kind; I was just returning the favor. She was my friend."

"A lot of people are shitty friends. You were a good one. Maybe her first."

"She always seemed like the expert."

"How expert could she have been? She was five. Sounds like the two of you were just what the other one needed."

"She was." I get quiet. I can feel myself about to cry. I try to shake it off. "So that day she's like, 'Come to recess,' and I tell her no, and we go back and forth about it and she goes, 'Fine, but then you have to come with me after school, and we're going to the playground. If you don't come, I'm telling everyone where you hide during recess.' So we go through the day and whatever, and then at the end during dismissal, we go outside and she makes straight for the swings. I know this is weird, but I'd never been on them before, or not that I remember. I'm sure my mom took me when I was little, but as soon as I was old enough to protest, I told her not to take me to the playground. I didn't like being with the other kids and I'd rather play in the yard at home or read in the park with her. So I got off to a rough start, but soon I was going as high as she was and just as fast. And I would look down and it was

59

brown legs over green grass and the school that barely seemed visible from up there and I'd look up and it'd be nothing but birds and clouds, and it seemed like I was up there looking down at us, and I just saw two girls with big smiles on their faces, I couldn't even tell them apart anymore, moving their legs in time and laughing. And she taught me how to jump off. And I was terrified. But she went and she was fine, and so I trusted her."

"Did you jump?"

"I did."

"How was it?"

"Perfect."

A bird comes to rest on the ledge above the window exactly over Dr. Katz's head, like it's come to perch on top of the two flyaway curls. It's a house finch; it's brown and yellow like they are, and female, I think. I like house finches; they're all over New York. They look like winged chipmunks, and I like how unfussy they seem, how small and how brave.

"So, what happened to Chocolate?"

"She never came back to school."

I cry for the rest of the session. I cry and watch the house finch come and go, come and go, and then just go.

8

I hate Tuesdays. Friday is really far away, and we have a double period of math after lunch. Mr. Garfield asked me for my homework again. I lied to him again, saying it was at home, or in the wrong folder, or whatever I told him today. He smiled and said no problem. I don't even know what the homework was.

The morning goes by okay. Ms. Smith has us do grammar exercises with sentences we've written in our journals. After grammar, we do silent reading for the last ten minutes of class, and I think about starting *The Perks of Being a Wallflower* but reread *Brown Girl Dreaming* instead. I know I should be reading something new, but it's like an old friend and I could use one of those right now. I sink into the book; it's not as good as Mom's shoulder, but it's close.

During lunch, I go eat in the bathroom. I don't even try the cafeteria. I don't even think of it as weird anymore. I try to shake the feeling that Mrs. Wexler is frowning at me. I just go to my stall, put my feet up so no one can see me, and take out my sandwich. It's not great, I guess, but it's better than the cafeteria with its lights and noise and human degradation. I like this stall because I like the graffiti in here the best. There are a few tags, *J.J. loves ME* and that kind of stuff, and there's this:

> *Do I dare to eat a peach?*
> *I shall wear white flannel trousers, and walk upon the beach.*
> *I hear the mermaids singing, each to each.*
> *I do not think that they will sing for me.*
> — *T. S. Eliot*

It's not that I love the poem, I mean I do, but it's mostly just nice to know that there's someone as weird as I am in this school. Someone who copies poetry about peaches on the bathroom wall. I imagine it's someone I haven't met yet, someone I somehow missed while I was hiding out in the ornithology stacks and they were tearing through poetry and memorizing lines. I try not to think that it's probably Leticia. Maybe it's someone who graduated, I tell myself; maybe it's someone I'll meet next year in high school. I know I'm a little old for imaginary friends, but I imagine that she ate lunch in here too. Peaches, obviously.

After lunch, Mr. Rothman drones on about the Silk Road. Maybe he's not droning. Maybe I just don't care. Either way, I watch birds out the window. I put my hands down by my sides, see if I can get them light, see if I can remember how it feels to be above all this. I close my eyes and feel my body go soft and light, and then I force myself to stop. I can't fly in the middle of social studies, no matter how boring it is. Anyway, he seems to have an announcement to make.

"So, there's going to be a talent show."

Mr. Rothman doesn't seem excited, but then again, I don't think he gets excited. The other kids in the class are, though. They start planning their routines immediately, Francis and Eric are talking about the magic tricks they want to perform, Naomi asks if she can sell cookies at the show to benefit charity, Destinee starts singing and Tracey tells her she sucks and then she tells Tracey she's fat, and this is all anybody is going to talk about for the next twenty minutes, so maybe I could have taken off. I get out my *National Geographic Complete Birds of North America* and read it under the table until the period ends.

When I get home it's only four and I get a text from Mom saying she won't be home until seven. I put on the Pixies and go out to the porch. It's almost April, and snow seems like a long time ago. So much seems like a long time ago. There are crocuses starting to poke through the dark earth. George from downstairs has already brought out my hammock. The bird feeder is empty; I fill it, letting a little bit drop on the ground near my feet, hoping it might get some bird to come and pick me up. It doesn't take long. She is small, brown-gray, skinny, and not as shy as she looks. A swamp sparrow — kind of how I've been feeling lately. I stare at her until I can feel the familiar rise of my arms, my belly rounded out beneath me, and up we go. I follow her lead, but I know where we're going. It's only a minute before we're sitting right at the top of the Brooklyn Bridge watching the traffic stall below. The honking sounds like a ringtone from this high up. It's just the two of us. It's never been like this before, I'm always part of a pack, but it's just us up here. I stare down too long, wondering if I can see George making his way home across the bridge on his bike, and I almost lose her as she takes off for our next spot, but my feet are fast and my arms are strong and then I'm right there with her, zooming above office buildings, doing curlicues around the letters in the Pepsi-Cola sign in Queens. We stop for a second on top of the *i*. There's a soccer game on Randall's Island. We fly higher, and I'm out of breath as we head farther north, Connecticut maybe? It's all bare trees and green grass. We keep going to an empty field with a big tree in the middle. I see more swamp sparrows as we get closer. Suddenly it's like the bird version of the cafeteria. I don't want to be in a pack today. This has never happened before, but I feel shy around them. I don't belong here. They take off in a V and I turn tail without looking back, back through the woods and the Pepsi-Cola sign, past the Brooklyn Bridge to my porch. Mom is standing in the kitchen staring at me. She sees me see her and comes out.

"Sparrow, you need to come inside now."

"Okay, I was just . . ."

"What?" She's expectant, even hopeful. Maybe I'll finally give her the answer she's been waiting months to hear. I try to think of something that won't sound crazy, that won't make her worry more. I don't think telling her that I just had this weird interaction with a family of birds in a tree in Connecticut will do it.

"Filling the feeder."

"I brought us sushi," she says, defeated.

My mom is a great cook, but lately she hasn't felt up to it. She puts miso soup in matching blue bowls and puts a California roll and a sweet potato tempura roll on a plate for me. She has sashimi and an eel roll. She always says that until I'm ready to eat eel, I can't really say I like sushi. She doesn't say that tonight. I put out napkins and the chopsticks Aunt Joan gave Mom for her birthday.

"Turn the music down please, Sparrow."

"Sorry." I turn it off.

"You didn't need to turn it off, just down. Who was it, anyway?"

"The Pixies."

"Where did you hear them?"

How do I explain? How do I tell my mother that my therapist is playing music for me because I refuse to talk to her too, but don't worry, it's helping.

"I don't know, around."

"How was school?"

"It was okay. There's going to be a talent show, which is like all anybody can talk about it and it's boring."

"Are you going to go?"

"No."

"You should think about it, Sparrow. You might have fun."

"Yeah, maybe. It's not until May."

We each turn our attention to our soy sauce, Mom taking a whole mound of wasabi and stirring it in. I poke the end of my chopstick into the wasabi so there's just a tiny hint of green on the tip and then stir that into my soy sauce. I see her smile at me, holding back a laugh. I smile back.

"You're almost in high school; you still think that a little wasabi will kill you?"

"No, that's exactly my point: A *little* wasabi won't." She laughs. It feels like I can breathe again.

"So," she says, taking a deep breath that takes away the new freedom my lungs have just found—I can tell this isn't going anywhere good—"what were you doing out on the porch?"

I drink my soup. I put a piece of sushi in my mouth. This has been so nice, this sitting here on our stools, closer to normal than we've been in almost two months. I hate what I'm about to do. I hate that I don't know what else to do. I hate that she'll blame herself.

"I said, filling the feeder."

"Sparrow, that's clearly not true. I watched you for thirty minutes; you were just standing there. You can tell me."

I have to find the teenage angst within me to push my stool away and storm upstairs. Really, I want to ask if I can sleep in her bed tonight, if we can watch whatever she wants until I fall asleep. If she'll read to me from *Persuasion*. If I can fall asleep on her shoulder with her arm around me.

I can't even get myself to slam my door. So close to normal, and then, just like that, we're back to this new, terrible normal where I'm stuck inside my room crying, listening to her downstairs cleaning up my dishes. I swear I can hear her sigh.

9

I'm cold and shivering when I come into the waiting room. It's been raining for days. You'd think by now I'd know to carry an umbrella. Mom is going to be pissed at me for not even bothering to put my hood up. At least, Old Mom would have been pissed. Current Mom is too scared of my flinging myself off a building to be mad at me. Honestly, nothing could be better for us at this point than for her to get really irritated with me like mothers are supposed to get with their daughters. I want her to roll her eyes, to say, *What on earth were you thinking? Don't you have any sense? You're going to catch a cold.* I want to roll my eyes right back and say, *Mom, I'm fine. Don't worry.* I want her to make me take a hot shower to warm up, like that'll keep me from getting sick; I want a fluffy robe and bad TV with my mom, who will forgive me when she sees me happy and healthy and wearing that much-too-big robe with the sleeves rolled over four times, like white terry-cloth swimmies. But I'm not fine, and she is worried, and those terry-cloth times seem as impossible to get to as Chocolate. Speaking of which, that's all Dr. Katz wants to talk about today.

"I don't want to talk about this anymore," I say, arms crossed.

"Well, you've tried the thing where you don't talk about how you feel. It's worked in some ways — you're still alive — but it hasn't in others, like that time about two months ago when everyone thought you were trying to kill yourself and you ended up in the hospital. We know what happens when you don't talk about it. What we don't know is what happens when you do."

"It's not going to make a difference."

"Might, might not."

"What am I supposed to talk about?"

"Why do you think it's been so hard to make a friend since Chocolate?"

I look down at my sneakers, knowing that the sky is no help to me today. There will be no house finches, there will be no goldfinches, no Cape May warblers, not even a pigeon.

I'm silent for a long time. It's not that I don't know the answer; it just seems stupid to say it. I am fourteen years old. Everyone in my life, my entire life, has told me that I just have to get over it, that only babies are scared, only babies long to be back in that noisy kindergarten hidden under backpacks and coats. Only babies would give anything for a swing set to send them flying away.

I'm convincing myself that I don't have to tell her. That therapy is just self-centered bullshit, there are starving children in Africa. That nothing that terrible has ever happened to me. That this is all a waste of time and money.

Just as I'm starting to really get on a roll, about to tell her off for real, I see myself in a long hallway, with many doors lining it, each holding a better treasure than the last. I start running down the hallway, and the faster I go, the faster the doors swing shut. Behind the first is my mom, and she looks less shocked than I want her to as the door slams in her face; the next has the guy from the Pixies playing "Where Is My Mind?" He doesn't even hear the door as it slams him inside the dark room. The next room is just sky, and birds. If I stepped in it, I could take flight, but I can't stop running and that door slams closed too. I am alone in a dark hallway full of closed doors.

"People, okay? I'm afraid of people," I say.

"That's right."

"And you think talking will fix that? Nothing is going to fix it."

"If I'm wrong, we already know what happens: Things stay the same. You know what that's like; you've been living it for the last fourteen years. The question is this—what if you never even try?"

A long, dark hallway with no birds, no Pixies. No people. What if I never even try.

"So, it's up to you. Let me know what you decide. I'll see you next week."

We have homeroom on Fridays. It's twenty minutes of forced bonding with fifteen other kids. Mostly I read. Sometimes Mr. Phillips will get on my case about it, but usually he leaves me alone. He's a fan of the one-on-one heart-to-heart "let-me-tell-you-a-little-something-Sparrow," but he's not a bad guy. He's the gym teacher when he's not running homeroom, he wears track pants every day, and they make a *swish swish swish* sound as he walks. He walks a lot when he's making a point, so homeroom tends to sound like "All right, guys" — *swish swish swish* — "today we're going to do some team building." *Swish swish swish.* Today we're doing Highs and Lows. Everyone sits in a circle and says the best and worst parts of their week. Some kids (Naomi) take it super seriously; they overshare about their dogs dying or their parents' divorce. Other kids are like, "The best part of my week is that there was creamed corn in the cafeteria." Mr. Phillips doesn't push it. He lets everyone say what they want; the only thing you can't do is pass.

As we go around the room and Jayce talks about how he beat a new level of whatever game, and Naomi talks about how the worst part of her week was that she got a pimple and has to go to the dermatologist and we all wonder why she wants us to know that, and Monique rolls her eyes at Sasha and mouths, "Loser," which Mr. Phillips doesn't see because he's looking at Naomi and trying to seem interested, and Travis says that the worst part of his week was babysitting his little brother, I try to think about what to say. The best part of my week was flying after school. The worst part was that my mom caught me and now thinks I'm even crazier than before. The best part was that I made progress in therapy. The worst part was that I'm in therapy. The best part was that my cousin, Curtis, gave me another iTunes gift card that I want to use to listen to the music we listen to in therapy. The worst part is contemplating saying that sentence out loud.

"Sparrow?"

"Um. The best part of my week was that my cousin gave me an iTunes gift card. The worst is that I hate creamed corn." Monique slivers her eyes at me. When Mr. Phillips turns his full, earnest attention to Brie, who is talking about her love for tempeh and how excited she is to work her parents' shift at the food co-op, Monique makes the she's-so-crazy sign, twirling her finger in a circle by her head, looking at Sasha and pointing at me. I don't care. It's not like she's wrong.

After our mandatory bonding, as we are filing out for lunch, Mr. Phillips stops me. "Sparrow, I need to see you for a minute, please." Is it about the creamed corn? Maybe he just wants to tell me I should really consider making more of an effort, getting to know some of the other kids, blah, blah, blah. Whatever it is, there is nothing in the world worse than standing around a classroom trying to look like everything is fine, waiting for everyone else to leave the room and for Jayce to quit fiddling with his stupid backpack so that some teacher can have their one-on-one heart-to-heart with you. Speaking of hearts, mine is beating *fast*.

Once we're alone, Mr. Phillips says, "Sparrow, what's going on? School? Classes? Homework?" My stomach is sinking with every word. "Kiddo, I know you've had a rough couple months, but you're not going to make it out of eighth grade if you don't start doing some work. You're such a smart girl, Sparrow—what are you doing?"

I don't know what to say. I have done every assignment I've ever had since I was five. I even kind of *liked* homework before. Well, you see, Mr. Phillips, between school and therapy and not talking to my mom, and turning into a bird and not sleeping, gadolinium hasn't been the first thing on my mind. I don't say that. I say:

"Okay."

"That's the thing, Sparrow, it *isn't* okay. You have two weeks to turn this around. Then I'm going to call your mom and we're going to have a parent-teacher conference."

I nod and leave, holding tight to the straps of my backpack. The next period has started, and there's no one in the halls. I run to the stairwell and make my way to the bathroom. There's a buzzing in my ear, a screeching kind of silence. I push through the very, very familiar door. I hear Mr. Phillips say "call your mom" over and over in my head and all I can think about is how much she's worried about me, and how much more she will be now. What's worse, so much worse, is that I can't fix it. I can't go home and sit down at the table and crank out math problems.

I walk home after school, looking everywhere for a bird—any kind—but it's like they've all left town. I feel a kind of lonely that's entirely different from the eat-lunch-in-the-bathroom kind. It's worse. Somewhere inside is the knowledge that they're never coming back. That I traded them in for just the idea of talking. That they know that I will eventually betray them, and so they've forgotten me. I try not to listen to this knowledge. I blare Alabama Shakes in my headphones to try to drown it out.

When I get home, Mom isn't there. She sends me a text: **Home late, problem with the server. I'm sorry. Order whatever you want! Love, Mom.** There's always a problem with the server. I go upstairs and lie down on my bed, surprised that I'm still crying, surprised that I have any tears left. I put the Pixies on again, and it's *With your feet on the air and your head on the ground* and I'm crying even harder. I curl into a ball on my bed. I can't bear to look out the window. I don't want to see the empty sky. Don't want to wait for them to come, knowing that they never will. I stay curled in a ball until the sun sets. I fall asleep, I guess, but *fall* isn't really the word. I plummet.

In my dream, for a minute, things are perfect. My body goes light and my arms go out, my heart swoops up and soars down; it's like it always is. But then I realize I'm on the ground. I stretch my wings—green and too thick—I run on my talons, gray, scaly, heavy, more like sneakers than like claws. I look, confused, at the bird that has come for me. I recognize its owl-like face, with its green and yellow feathers and its enormous gray beak that looks just like a nose. It's a kakapo. I must be dreaming; they're rare birds found only in New Zealand and practically extinct by now. Also, they're flightless. They live in the forest and flap their wings and go absolutely nowhere. I know this, and it doesn't stop me. I'm on the stoop outside my house flapping my wings and running with my heavy talons and going nowhere.

In my dream, George comes outside from downstairs and says, "Where are you going?" and then I hear Mom laugh. Her laugh turns into a cry and I am up in the air finally, but I'm not a kakapo anymore. My wings are strong and light gray-brown. I look down at my white chest. I swoop in a familiar loop in the sky, taking my time, enjoying the sun on my face, but I can't shake the feeling that something is very, very wrong. I want to enjoy the flight, I want to enjoy the view and the soaring and the wind, I want to feel how easy it is breathing through a beak.

We have flown north to Albany; I recognize the capitol building from a trip there in elementary school. That's not why we're here, though. I feel dread climbing its way up my body. I am headed for an enormous landfill, as if my chest were being pulled from the sky to the ground. I'm not headed for the trash, I see now, but for a small, skinny dog wandering the heap. That's when I look at my wings and understand — the light grayish brown, the white underbelly, the soaring in circles. A vulture. That dog is supposed to be my dinner. I try to keep myself in the air, anything to keep that dog from ending up between my talons. As I get closer and closer, my feathers begin to fall out, first one by one, and then in clumps, until I can see my bones. Below me, I see my right talon fall off my body to the ground. Then my left. I hear the *thunk* they make as they land in the pile of trash, becoming a snack for the junkyard dog. A strong wind comes, and all my belly feathers are gone. I'm a pile of bones in the air. Suddenly, I'm headed straight for the Brooklyn Bridge. I crash headfirst into the bricks and crumble to dust in the water. Then I wake up.

I can't breathe. Beak or no beak, I can't breathe. It's a dream, I tell myself, but it doesn't help. I get out of the too-hot bed with its clinging covers. I open the window. It's not enough. I feel stuck, like there's not enough air in my room. I run down the hall to the bathroom. I splash water on my face. It feels hot even though it's cold. I can't catch my breath. I feel like my face is on fire and nothing can put out the flames. I don't hear Mom knock, but all of a sudden her hand is on my back.

"Sparrow," she says, and her voice puts the flames out. "Sparrow, it's okay."

I look her in the eyes; mine are wide, I can tell. I can't breathe. She takes my hands.

"Breathe with me. You had a bad dream. Just breathe." I follow her breath, and then she pulls me to her and holds me there.

76

"Little Sparrow," she says, "you're okay."

I don't think so, and I bet she doesn't think so either, but I'll take it. I start to breathe again. She walks me back to my room and makes my bed for me, shaking out the crumpled sheets and smoothing the duvet. She fluffs the pillows. Mom likes a bed just so.

"Come now," she says, and I get in. The sheets feel cool now, and the breeze through the window feels good on my damp forehead. She sits on the edge of my bed, and I roll over to face the wall. She is rubbing my back until I fall asleep, like I'm five years old. Then again, I just woke my mom up with a nightmare, so five sounds about right.

"Mom?" I say.

"Yes, Sparrow?"

"Stay."

I wish that had changed everything, but once daylight hits, we get weird again. I go downstairs for breakfast, and Mom makes me eggs and some tea and I pick at the eggs and drink the tea.

"You feeling better?" she asks, her voice nearly shaking with worry.

"Yeah, Mom, I'm fine," I say, sounding lifeless even to my own ears. I can't even reassure myself.

"Okay, well, if you want to talk."

"It was just a bad dream."

And then there it is, our new, terrible silent routine. And to top it off, I have no birds and the world feels like a different kind of dark than it felt before. Mom isn't perfect, but I miss her. I miss her picky neatness, I miss her bothering me about taking my nose out of a book and making a friend for once, I miss her getting on my case about my hair. I miss telling her about what I'm reading, what I'm thinking, asking her about work, listening to her carry on about Aunt Joan and whatever drama she's gotten into. I miss her. There is a sadness I can't shake, that's not just from breakfast. There are no birds by the feeder. There aren't pigeons cluttering the sidewalk as I go to school. I know, now, that last night's dream was the last flight I'll take.

Maybe Dr. Katz will be sick today, maybe she'll be sick forever, maybe she'll decide she doesn't want to waste her time on nutcases like me anymore, maybe she'll say, "Listen, Sparrow, some people are just fine. You're one of them. Off you go." I think terrible things. I think, Maybe she was in an accident. I think, Maybe she's dead.

"Sparrow." She appears at the door, perfectly healthy, in a white linen shirt rolled to her elbows with a red striped shirt underneath and black jeans. I can see her tattoo fully now; it's a ring of black waves that goes all around her forearm.

"Hi," I say.

I walk through the door and to my chair. This is habit by

now; I do it the way I do math class, not because I want to, not because I understand it, but because my body knows what to do and does it without my approval. I am sitting. I am waiting. I am not making eye contact.

"How are you over there?"

"I'm okay." There are no birds. I am nothing like okay.

"You don't seem so okay."

"I guess I'm a liar, then."

"Sparrow."

I'm done. Forget this woman. I can't look out the window, I won't see any birds, and the loneliness will swallow me up and I'll die. I'll stick to my shoes on the carpet.

"Can we just listen to music, please?" I am all snarl and growl today. Get. Away. From. Me.

"I think we have to talk a little, Sparrow."

"I'm scared, okay?" I spit the words out of my mouth.

"Yeah, that's okay. Of what?"

I shake my head slowly. I have to control my body to keep myself from rocking back and forth like those kids you see in the Orphans of the World infomercials or whatever. For one dollar a day, you can make a difference in this child's life. Picture of a skinny, miserable, rocking child, flies near her mouth. That's me, minus the flies.

"Does it feel like this is going to kill you?"

Yes, I think. But I say, "That's stupid."

"Sparrow, does it feel like this is going to kill you?"

"It feels like it already has."

"Okay."

She presses play on her iPod. I let myself think that she's going to lay off, to give me a freaking break already, but not this lady. There's something coming.

The piano is first, banging but controlled. Like it's only hinting at all the anger underneath. Like if she — before I hear the voice, I know this is a she — if she let it all out, the stereo would explode.

Is the first word *pissing*? It is. Damn, Dr. Katz.

I like the moaning in her voice. I like that she doesn't sound like a woman. It's not that she sounds like a man; it's like she sounds like something way beyond silly signs on a bathroom door. It's human. It's animal.

I'm crying. I want the birds to come back. I want Mom to come back. I want Mrs. Wexler to come back. I want Chocolate to come back. I want to come back. I curl my legs under me. No one can make a difference in this child's life. Here, the world says: love things, lose them, good luck. The woman cries through the stereo. *What about it?*

It's an accident, the look I give her, straight at her face.

"I HATE THIS," I shout across the music.

"This what?"

"THIS. THIS. THIS ALL OF THIS," I shout, and I keep shouting, "I hate Mom, I hate school, I hate therapy, I hate that anyone found me on that stupid roof, I hate that Chocolate's gone, I hate that Mrs. Wexler's dead and I hate that I was doing fine until two months ago and now I'm worse off than ever and if I could just fly, I'd be fine, but I can't even do that anymore because the birds are gone."

I know I'm screwed. I know I have said way too much, and said it in the craziest way possible. And the music is over, and now it's just me and this woman and our chairs. Except I am standing. Why am I standing? I sit.

"Okay," she says. "Now we can get somewhere."

"Oh, well, hey, as long as I'm making your job easier," I hiss through my teeth.

"Now you get to feel better. You've got a lot to say, Sparrow, and when you keep it inside for as long as you have, it's going to do a whole lot of damage. And getting it out isn't easy, or painless."

I close my eyes. I see walls coming down around me, they are thick bricks that rise over Dr. Katz's face, I see her eyes like she wants to say something to me but then the bricks cover them and she's gone. I am in a dark brick room, and I can't hear her voice, I can't see anything, it's just me in here, and it's safe. It's not as fun as flying, but it's better than sitting in this terrible room with this terrible woman who thinks she knows me.

Eventually I hear her voice. "Sparrow, you've shut down. That's okay. We can try again next week." I want to think, Fat freaking chance, I want to think, You're never going to see me again. Instead, I'm just surprised to hear the voice on this side of the wall. Surprised that she somehow made her way in here. And maybe a little relieved.

10

In English today, we get to listen to music during reading. We're only allowed to on Fridays, and I've never taken advantage of it before, but I do today—I just downloaded a White Stripes album onto my iPod. I'm listening to them and holding *The Perks of Being a Wallflower* in my hand. I turn the music up and crack the cover. A flyer falls out. It's bright blue and purple and says *Gertrude Nix Rock Camp for Girls*, with pictures of girls screaming into microphones, guitars weighing down their shoulders, drumsticks flying. It's a monthlong sleepaway camp for eight- to sixteen-year-old girls. My throat tightens. I wonder if this is Mrs. Wexler's last attempt to get me to open my mouth and make a friend. Missing her comes like a wave, fast and unstoppable. I can't cry. Not here. I stuff the flyer into my backpack and go back to my book.

"Hi!" Mom shouts when she comes in my room, and I finally turn around.

"Oh, hey," I say, glued to the screen. She reaches over and turns down the volume, which is annoying but also parental, and it feels good to have her be annoying instead of worried and sad.

"What is this?"

"Sonic Youth," I say.

"Okay," she says. "How'd you hear about them?"

"School," I say, trying to sound natural, trying to sound like my sudden interest in the old-school indie rock is what all the brown girls are doing these days.

"A friend?"

"I don't know."

"A boy?"

"No, Mom."

"Okay, okay. Dinner in fifteen minutes."

She heads downstairs, and I'm grateful for the mildly normal interaction, though I'm pretty sure that once we sit through dinner, things will be all awkward again. Soon the smell of macaroni and cheese wafts up to me and carries me downstairs by the nose.

"It smells good, Mom," I say. Macaroni and cheese is my favorite, how she makes it, hot and gooey from the oven, four different kinds of cheese, and bread crumbs brown and crunchy on top. She takes a kale salad out of the refrigerator, for balance, I guess.

"Good," she says. "Set the table." This feels normal. I feel nervous. I put two plates on the island and try to grab the forks, napkins, and glasses in one hand — she would call it a lazy man's load.

"How was your day?" she asks.

"Okay," I say. "Yours?"

"It was busy. You know, too much work."

"As always." I smile. This feels good.

"Did you want to go to Central Park some weekend soon?" Central Park. Where we always go when springtime comes on strong. I sit and read and "watch" the birds (she thinks I'm only watching), and she reads. We have an actual picnic basket and everything. It's usually my favorite thing. It's like how most kids feel about Disneyland. I don't know about this year. It might be too sad, since I'm obviously never going to get to fly again.

"Um, maybe," I say, trying to keep the normal going. I have to put my fork down, though. The thought of sitting on the ground looking up for the rest of my life ruins my appetite.

"You don't want to?"

"We'll see." There it is — the weird blanket of tension that settles in on both of us, my mother thinking, probably, that I don't want to spend time with her, me thinking about the fact that I turn into a bird and am totally, certifiably crazy and she has no idea. She just wants to go to the park. Because I like the park. Or did. And because she loves me. Or did.

"Maybe a movie?" I suggest, trying hard to sound light, bright, happy.

"Sure," she says, unsure. I've ruined everything. Again. We

don't speak for the rest of the meal, which isn't much longer, since I'm just picking at my mac and cheese now and she seems to have lost interest in her kale salad.

"Do you want to watch TV?" I ask.

"I should really work," she says. I look down. I say nothing. I'm not trying to guilt-trip her, I'm just trying to figure out how we're ever going to stop being such strangers to each other.

"Maybe just for a little while," she says.

"You pick," I say, putting our dishes in the sink and heading through the swing door. She picks some show about doctors who love each other and work too much, and I don't know what's happening or care too much, but I'm pretty happy to be sitting on the couch with Mom like she's Mom and not just some lady I live with.

On the show, one doctor is trying to save this woman's life but the woman keeps insisting that she has nothing left to live for. I fall asleep, but I'm pretty sure that in the last five minutes her long-lost kids all come in and she finds her will to live. I don't know what I dream about, but when I wake up gasping, I hear the sound of crushed bones in my ears — is it the TV? My mouth tastes like dirt, and my throat feels scratched and dry, like there's something stuck in it — a feather? That'd be so predictable. I hate that this is the closest I'll get to flying again. I hate that Mom is rushing to get me a glass of water and then she'll ask me what I dreamt about and I'll say I don't know and she'll ask if I'm okay and I'll say yeah, and then we'll go back to watching this show, and when I go to bed later, I'll have trouble falling asleep and I'll hate waking up because my mouth will taste like dirt and feathers and I won't even remember the fall.

PART 2

11

My iPod is going so loud I barely hear Dr. Katz when she opens the door. I've been listening to "Pissing in a River" on repeat. I've used up almost all of Curtis's gift cards by now. He's been giving me iTunes gift cards for the last maybe five Christmases, birthdays, whatevers. It's like he's begging me, *Please, cousin, get cool, try a little bit.* I give him Amazon gift cards: *Please, cousin, read something, try a little bit.* I don't think he's ever used one of mine, but I'm using his now. I doubt Patti Smith and Alabama Shakes and the Pixies on repeat were what he had in mind, but I don't care. Cool isn't what I'm looking for. I'm looking for the ache they all have. The map in their voices that leads to the place where I live, the place I didn't know anyone else knew how to get to.

Gold Pumas, today, I notice, as she sits down. A little lightning-bolt earring in one ear and a small gold hoop in the other. She means business. Silence. From both of us. Expectant eyebrows over her silver glasses, the middle part of her hair, go up to the ceiling. I consider the window. Still no birds. They must have gotten the message: I got my wings clipped.

"You know where to start," she says.

"Last week?"

She nods. "Last week. We need to talk about some things—that's for sure. But for now, let's start with the big question."

"Which one?"

"Why were you on the rooftop?"

"I wasn't trying to kill myself."

"That much is clear."

"This is going to sound crazy."

"Sparrow, I'm a therapist. You think you might let me be the judge of crazy?"

"You can't tell Mom."

"Did it involve hurting yourself or others?"

"No. Not really. I mean, I know people thought I was trying to hurt myself, but I wasn't."

"Then there's no reason I'd have to share any of this with your mother."

I want to time this right. It's 3:35. We stop at 3:50. I don't want to have too much time at the end for her to call the nuthouse or ask me how telling her makes me feel. I can say it and bolt. Perfect.

"Killing time over there?" she asks, a smile in her voice.

Ugh. I hate it when she knows. I don't even pretend. "Yeah."

"You know, this is the hard part. The part before you say it. The part after is just a little easier, mostly because you're not waiting to do the hardest thing you've ever done."

Fine. Fine. Fine. Fine. Fine. Fine. Fine. Fine. Fine. Fine. Fine.

Fine. Fine. Fine. Fine. Like Patti Smith would say, What about it. What about it. What about it. What about it.

"I was going to fly, okay?"

"Okay." She's right there. She's saying *Okay* like *Do you want some tea?* Like this isn't surprising, like she knew all along, like she's heard crazier things, like this isn't crazy to her at all, like it's just true.

"Do you fly a lot?"

"Um. Yeah. I guess. I used to."

"But the birds aren't around anymore?"

"Not for a few weeks. How did you know?"

"You said something about them last week." True. I forgot that. The whole session is kind of gray and blurry, like an old whiteboard, the notes from last class erased but still showing through.

"Do you think I'm crazy? Am I crazy?"

"No."

"No *but*, is what you mean."

"Is it?"

"Who thinks they can fly?"

"You do."

"Yeah, me and crazy people."

"I think that's the easy answer. Here's what I know, Sparrow—you're not crazy. You might feel crazy at times; I think all human beings who are paying any kind of attention think that they must be crazy. Sometimes we have to find ways to deal with the crazy things around us, and those can make us feel crazier, or they can make us feel safe. Wanting to feel safe doesn't make you crazy; it makes you a human being, even when you'd rather be a bird."

"Okay." I can't look at her, but I want to. I want her to see that if she's not telling me the truth, my world is going to fall apart at the seams. I want her to see that no one has even come close to this secret. I want her to know that she better not be lying. I want her to know that even though I feel like I might throw up right here on her rug, I also feel just a little better. I stare at the gold Pumas instead.

Somewhere deep, deep inside of me, something begins to warm up. Something I never knew was cold to begin with.

12

That weekend, we don't go to the park, but we do ride bikes down to the pier at Red Hook. Mom wants to do some grocery shopping at the Fairway, and I'm happy to sit on the bench outside and watch the water. All I can see are seagulls, of course, and they can't see me anymore, but there's something nice about sitting on the bench with sun on my face and the breeze from the water rising up to greet me. It's not flying, but it's nice. Mom comes out and sits beside me, her bag full of groceries.

"Hi there," she says.

"Hi. I was just thinking about this bike ride we had to take when you made me go to that weird Y camp. Do you remember that? We rode all the way down here."

"I'm surprised you remember it. That was years ago."

"Who could forget a death ride to Red Hook with thirty other eight-year-olds in the middle of summer?"

"So dramatic, my daughter."

"It was awful!"

"Was it as awful as the overnight?"

"Well, I wouldn't know, would I?" I grinned at her, just a little. The Y camp was awful—lots of team sports and swimming and walks through different parks in the city. Did I mention the team sports? Lots of them. But the worst part was the overnight. They took all us city kids upstate to "get some fresh air" and "practice wilderness skills." I lasted exactly the length of the bus ride. We got there and they showed us the tarps on the ground that we were supposed to magically turn into tents. I was with a bunch of girls who had been separated from their other friends, who were in another tent. One of them came over to express her condolences that they'd be stuck with the weird, quiet girl, and said she hoped they'd have fun reading books all day. Then a mosquito bit me. Then I called Mom to come get me.

I sat on a bench by the entrance to the campsite and read a book until it was dark. While I was waiting, Jacob came and sat down next to me. I didn't really know Jacob—he wasn't much of a talker either. I knew he was from Queens, and wasn't very good at sports, and that was about it. He had dreads that fell in his face, mostly because he was always looking down, and he had high cheekbones and big eyes. He looked delicate, like he could break if you touched him, and kind of beautiful, which I didn't know boys could be. He was short for eight and his basketball jersey sat uncomfortably on his shoulders, like he hadn't chosen it. He climbed onto the rock next to the bench I was sitting on.

"Hi," he said. He had never spoken a single word to me before. Now he was sitting here like we were old friends.

"Hey, Jacob."

"You're leaving?"

"Definitely."

He looked down for a second, his hair covering his entire face, and then straight up to the sky. "I want to leave."

"You should."

"My dad won't let me."

"Why not?"

"He's the one who sends me to this stupid camp in the first place. 'It's about time you learned to play something other than video games, son,' " he said, shoulders back, trying to lower his voice to imitate his dad, who I could tell was a tall man.

"Yeah, my cousin plays a lot of video games. My aunt is always trying to get him outside."

"I don't like video games; that's just what he thinks. I'm sitting in my room reading and drawing."

"Why don't you tell him that?"

"Yeah, right. My dad would think that was even worse, spending all that time on sissy stuff." He looked embarrassed.

"I don't think it's sissy. I like drawing too."

"You're a girl!"

"So?"

"So, girls are supposed to draw and like books."

"Right, and you're supposed to like dirt and sports because you're a boy. That's dumb."

"Maybe I'm not a boy. I don't want to be a basketball star."

"What do you want to be?"

He got quiet quiet and looked like he might cry. "It's dumb."

"Tell me."

"A poet."

"I think you'd be a good poet."

"Why?"

"Because you're not what you seem."

His smile took up nearly his entire face. "You read a lot, huh?"

"Yeah. Who are your favorite poets?"

"I like Nikki Giovanni and Countee Cullen. Shel Silverstein too, but that's kid stuff."

"I haven't heard of them."

"You should read them. What do you like to read?"

"I'm reading *The Watsons Go to Birmingham* right now. My favorite book is *Harriet the Spy*."

"I like those."

"Cool."

We both got quiet, like we just realized that we were having a conversation with a total stranger who maybe didn't feel so much like a stranger anymore.

"I should go back, I guess. They might notice I'm gone," Jacob said.

"They might?"

"It's not like I take up a lot of space."

"I know what you mean."

"I really wish I could leave like you."

"It's only one night. You'll be okay."

"Did that work when they said it to you?"

I smiled. "Not even a little." He jumped off his rock and started to head back toward camp.

"Hey, Sparrow," he called over his shoulder.

"Yeah?"

"What do you want to be when you grow up?"

Why not try the truth? "A bird."

"Cool. You'll be good at that. Bye."

"Bye."

I sat there and watched as the owls and the nightjars took their positions. The only thing better than the owl's hooting was the roar of my mother's engine as she pulled into the campsite. She gave me a big hug, no questions asked, and drove me to the nearest diner. I got macaroni and cheese and she got a root beer float, and we drove back home to the superior wilds of Brooklyn. I never went back to the camp.

I spent the rest of the summer at Aunt Joan's with Curtis. They basically let me read all summer. It was great, but I never got to see Jacob again. I hope he's okay. I hope the world hasn't knocked the poet out of him yet. Thinking about that summer, about Mom driving three hours to come and bring me home because she wouldn't leave me in a tent with evil girls and mosquitoes, about our diner dinner and our long ride home, makes my heart lift just a little.

We're about to get back on our bikes when I decide to go for it. I give her a big hug. It's been so long that I'm taller in our hug than I used to be. My head is at her shoulder.

"Thanks for coming to get me," I say.

"It was a long time ago, honey. But you're welcome. Anytime."

We ride home, my legs burning as we go up the hill to our house, Mom going strong despite the heavy load strapped to her back.

13

The tally: Eleven weeks since the rooftop. Three weeks since my last flight. One week since I told Dr. Katz about flying. Eleven weeks since I've touched any homework, and three since Mr. Phillips said he would call my mom. I hope he forgot. Eleven weeks of weird weird weird with me and Mom. I hate that this sad, I-give-up silence between us is normal, that our hug on Saturday is the strange thing. Still, though, that hug was nice. Maybe it's just because winter is over and gray March has marched on, but things feel a little lighter. Like there's more room inside me.

"Hi, Sparrow, come on in."

I settle in across from Dr. K and let out a deep breath. "So, things are still messed up—I know it's not normal to want to fly, even if you're not lying and I'm not crazy, and things are still weird at home and I still hate school, but I slept better this past week."

"How 'bout that," she says, pleased.

"Maybe I feel better because I finally told someone?"

"Yeah, maybe."

"And because you didn't say I was a freak, even though I'm pretty sure that I am."

"So, tell me about it."

"About being a freak?"

"You're not a freak. Tell me about flying."

"Well, you see, when birds stretch their wings, they go up to the sky and—"

"Yes, thank you. I know what the word means. When did you start flying?"

"I already told you about that."

She thinks for a moment. "On the swings with Chocolate?"

"Yeah, I think so. I mean, that's the first time I had the feeling. But it's different because I was actually in the air, I was actually flying. And I didn't turn into a bird that time, I was just me."

"When was the first time you turned into a bird?"

"The day after Chocolate left."

"What happened?"

"My mom was late. She's always late. I told her what happened, and she said, 'Well, you'll just have to make a new friend.' Like it was easy, like it was nothing. I know that it should be, but it's not for me. It never has been. Anyway, I went to my room, and I cried and cried. I got into bed and pulled the sheets over my head, and I lay as still as I could. I wanted to disappear."

"And then it happened?"

"Yeah. I remembered flying off the swings with Chocolate

the day before. I closed my eyes, and I could feel my heart swoop up and then back down like it did when I let go of the chains of the swing. I could feel my legs ungrounded. But instead of landing, like I did the day before, I kept going. My arms got wide and smooth alongside my body. My legs went up under me, ready for a landing but curled for flight. Wind to my face. I went up into blue and didn't look back. I didn't open my eyes until the next morning. I stopped crying about Chocolate after that, mostly. I just flew. I've been flying since. Until three weeks ago."

"What happened three weeks ago?"

"The birds stopped coming for me."

"So, a bird would come by and get you and you would leave with it?"

"Yeah, normally. And then I betrayed them, and they stopped."

"How so?"

"It was the day you basically told me I could be screwed up forever or I could talk. I decided to talk. I haven't flown since. There haven't even been any birds. It's like they haven't just left me; they left the entire city."

"Is it lonely?"

I can't believe this is what she's asking. She doesn't seem freaked out by the fact that I look for birds to pick me up and take me away. That I've seen my own body covered in feathers and soaring through clouds.

"It's not like I have a lot of other people to spend time with."

"So you said that everything would be okay if you could just fly, but you can't even do that anymore because the birds are gone?"

"I said that?"

"Yes."

"When?"

"When we listened to 'Pissing in a River.'"

"What, do you have a tape recorder?"

"You don't remember, do you?"

"No."

"That's okay."

"Why don't I remember?"

"It happens sometimes. Our brains will short out so that we can do whatever we're doing even though we're terrified."

"Oh." Well, that just about explains my whole life.

"So, have you ever told anyone about flying?"

"Would you have? If you thought you were crazy, would you just go around chatting about it? Hey, I'm Sparrow, also, I turn into a bird, cool, huh?"

"Probably not."

"Right. So, no, I never told anyone."

"Not your mom?"

"No."

"So, how's life on the ground?"

"I don't like it. The worst part was when the birds just stopped coming. I felt dead. I bet you think I'm exaggerating or being a drama queen or something but that's how I felt."

She lets out a laugh. Awesome, she must think I'm ridiculous.

"Sparrow, you don't speak nearly enough to be a drama queen. And the only thing that ever made you feel alive was gone, so it makes sense that you didn't feel very alive."

I miss them. *Miss* isn't the right word. I miss them the way you miss water in a desert. I miss them the way children miss their parents, the way I miss Mrs. Wexler, the way I miss things being easy and clouds being below me. The way you miss things you don't know how to be without, but you know they're never coming back.

14

Mrs. Wexler's funeral was the Friday after her accident. Mom helped me buy a black dress. I let her do my hair, I didn't just put it up in a poof like I usually do. I sat with my back against the couch as she sat above me, comb in hand, towel on my shoulders. She made two plaits on either side, milkmaid braids is what she calls them. It felt like being a little kid again, I'm just as tender-headed as I was then, but it felt kind of good too, even if it was the saddest day of my life. I guess it was that feeling of being a little girl on the rug getting my hair combed by my mom that made me tell her where I'd been eating lunch for the last three years. I took a deep breath.

"Don't be mad," I said, picking at the rug, "but I've been eating lunch in the library."

"Mmm. For how long?" Mom didn't know that she didn't know everything about me.

"Since fifth grade."

Her strong, steady hands in my hair paused. I felt her shoulders sag as she sighed.

"Why didn't you tell me?"

"I knew what you'd say."

"What's that?"

"That I should spend more time with people and less time with books. But you don't understand—"

"I do understand, Sparrow." I felt the soft tug of her hands finishing a plait. "I just want you to challenge yourself."

"I made a friend in the library."

"Really?"

"Yeah, that's where I met Leticia."

"That's great, baby."

"But I don't think we're friends anymore."

"Why not?"

"I don't know. I wanted to go to the funeral with her, but I don't think she's going." Mom started the braid on the other side and I had to hold my ear to my shoulder for what felt like forever. "Mom?"

"Mmm?"

"Will you go with me?"

"Of course." Her voice cracked. I knew I'd ruin my hair if I turned around to look at her, and I knew she didn't want me to. I stared straight ahead and wondered why Mrs. Wexler's death seemed to have Mom as upset as it had me.

That's what I'm thinking about as I watch Mom rustling around the kitchen trying to get ready for work. She's wearing the same dress she wore to the funeral. I'll never wear my black dress again. Mom looks good in hers, but just seeing it makes me sad. I sip my tea and wish she would sit down and eat with me, but I know she has to get out the door. She sees me staring at her.

"What is it, Sparrow?" Mom in a rush is not the epitome of patience.

"Nothing, sorry." I look at my tea. She sighs, and it sounds like *ugh*. I tell my face not to react, but I can feel my mouth pulling down at the corners anyway and my face getting hot. She turns her back as she finishes pouring a thermos full of tea and throws a granola bar into her briefcase.

"I'll see you late," she says. She approaches me, and I can tell she's trying to decide if she's going for a hug or a kiss on the cheek or what. She ends up patting my shoulder and it's all the definition of awkward. I leave right after her for school. We could've left together but I don't think either of us wanted that.

15

"Hi, Sparrow, come on in."

I like this part, the little rush at the beginning. I take in what she's wearing (olive cargo pants, Converse, a loose-fitting black shirt), silently judge it, like her anyway, sit down, wait for her to sit down; this part is the easy part. We start talking about music. Easy. I tell her about Curtis and the gift cards and listening to Alabama Shakes and the Pixies and Patti Smith all the time.

I can't tell her the rest, that I'm hungry for more — that these people seem to be keeping me company now that the birds are gone.

"So, tell me about the birds."

"What does that have to do with music?" She looks at me like, *You know.* I do know. "Because that's what's keeping me company now." She smiles. "Fine. What about them?"

"When did you turn into a bird?"

"I mean, a lot. I don't know."

"Like when?"

"Like all the time!"

"Give me three."

"Ugh. Fine. How about every day I went into the cafeteria before fifth grade and all this year?"

"What happened in fifth grade?"

"I started to eat lunch in the library with Mrs. Wexler."

"And then she died?"

"Yeah, this October."

"So, why did you hate lunch before that?"

"Have you ever been in a cafeteria? It's horrible."

"As I recall, they can be pretty stressful places. Why did yours make you call on the birds?"

"Well, you can't fly in a cafeteria, obviously, but the only thing that made lunch okay was knowing that we'd go to recess for fifteen minutes, and I'd get to fly at least for a little bit."

"Why was it so bad?"

"Why are you so nosy?"

"Sparrow."

"What?" My arms are crossed. My legs are crossed. I can feel myself squirming in my chair. I want to leave.

"Why did you hate lunch?"

"Why do you think?" Silence. Expectant eyebrows. Is she for real? "Monique."

"Who's Monique?"

"She's Leticia's friend."

"Who's Leticia?"

"She was my friend, or at least I think she was my friend. We were in Mrs. Wexler's reading group together. We liked a lot of the same books. We spent lunch together in the library every day until Mrs. Wexler died." '

"Then what happened?"

"I had to go back to the cafeteria. I haven't eaten in the cafeteria since the first week of fifth grade. So everyone has their spots to sit in, the geek boys, the not-so-popular girls, the jock boys, and the popular girls, and Monique was their queen. I stood there trying to figure out where I could sit and not bother anyone and not be bothered by anyone. That's when I saw Leticia. There was a seat right next to her. I walked up to her table, and she said hi and moved over so I could sit and I ended up sitting between her and Monique. We talked a little about some books we liked, and the whole time Monique was moving her elbows out so I had less and less room and saying, 'What are you guys talking about?' Leticia said, 'Nothing.' I don't know why she didn't just tell her we were talking about books. I ate my lunch as fast as I could, but it didn't matter because we weren't allowed to leave. Leticia didn't talk to me much after that; she mostly talked to the other kids at the table. But she was the only person I knew, so I kept sitting there for the rest of the week."

"And what were they talking about?"

"It depended on the day. Sometimes they talked about boys. Sometimes it was about how weird it was that I was sitting with them. Sometimes it was about how I thought I was better than they were because I knew the right answer in class and did my freaking homework. And then there was the terrible day."

"What was that?"

"The day my mother packed Oreos in my lunch. She's a health nut. It was supposed to be a nice surprise."

Dr. Katz sighs, and closes her eyes; she knows what's about to come. "Oh, no."

"Yeah. I opened them up and Monique just starts shrieking, 'Look, look, the Oreo brought Oreos! The Oreo brought Oreos!'"

"That sucks. Monique sucks."

"Whatever. Girls like her don't like me. I read books and don't listen to Nicki Minaj. I'm 'stuck up.'"

"What did Leticia say?"

I look down. I shake my head. I can't get myself to say the truth—that she said nothing. I hate thinking about it. Hate thinking about her there, laughing with those girls like she never sat on a rug with me in the corner of the library crying about our favorite sad part in a book.

"Did you tell a teacher about what they were doing?"

"No. I told my mom."

"And what did she say?"

"That they're just jealous. I have no idea what they'd be jealous of. They think I'm stuck up because I don't talk to them, but I don't talk to *anyone*. And they think I'm a snob because I read all the time. They'd read too if they never talked. Black girls just don't like me."

"This one does." Shelikesmeshelikesme.

"You don't go to my school, though."

"You think all the black girls at your school are like that? Even the not-so-populars?"

"They aren't mean to me, but they probably think the same thing. That I'm a weirdo who doesn't have any friends. I mean, they'd be right."

"So, what happened next?"

"I looked up to the windows. There were only a few, right at the top. And I waited for a bird to fly by, and as soon as one did, it started. My skin went cold like goose bumps, but I felt so warm inside, and I felt feathers come, very, very slowly. My bones went light; my face shifted shape. Then I could hang on until we'd be dismissed for recess."

"And what would happen at recess?"

"I'd find a corner where no one was and sit down on a bench. I'd stare up, and I'd wait. Fifteen minutes isn't long, but it's enough. I'd feel my body go up, and I'd join whichever family of birds was closest by—a warbler in the spring or purple finch in the fall or once a northern goshawk—and my feathers would turn the color of their feathers, my feet would go under me, and I'd have that *swoop swoop* feeling in my heart, and I'd be very, very far away from those girls and those boys and the school and everything."

"Where would you fly?"

"Wherever they were going, as far as I could get in fifteen minutes. Over all of Brooklyn, the park, the river, northeast over traffic on the BQE, sometimes to Staten Island, even, to look at the houses and the lawns."

"Northeast on the BQE, huh?"

"Yeah. When I still had Mrs. Wexler, I spent a lot of time reading maps and figuring out where we were going. Once I flew over Governors Island, before they remade it into a picnic area and it still looked like the set of a horror movie, and once I sat on top of the crown of the Statue of Liberty."

"Sounds like a better recess than most people get."

"I don't know. Maybe hanging out with your friends is like that for other people."

"Maybe. When else would you fly?"

"When Mrs. Wexler died."

"I bet. When else?"

"Sometimes when we had to go to my aunt's for holidays."

"When else?"

"My birthday."

"When else?'

"When these kids on my block called me a stuck-up bitch."

"When else?"

"Well, there was that time on the roof about two months back, not sure if you heard about that."

"Ha!" She smiles. I smile back. I like making her laugh.

"And what led to that?" she asks.

"I'm sorry, Dr. Katz, that's all we have time for this week," I say, half joking, half praying I'm right.

"Nice try, Sparrow," she says, sneaking a look at her watch.

"Oh! You're right. Okay. I'll see you next week." I get up to go.

"By the way," she asks, "have you ever heard of TV on the Radio?"

"No."

"You might check them out."

That night, I'm blaring TV on the Radio at home. Dr. Katz isn't wrong—I love them. My knees are making my computer screen bounce; my feet can't sit still. I watch videos of them on YouTube and can't help but think that if they'd been eating lunch with me that day with Monique, they would have said something. When Mom comes home, she reaches over and turns off my speakers in the middle of "Happy Idiot" and I don't even get a chance to tell her about them. She says, "We need to talk." I nod without turning around, my stomach in knots.

"Mr. Phillips called." I nod again. I guess he didn't forget. "Sparrow, turn around when I'm talking to you." I spin my chair toward her. "He says I need to come in. Do you know what it's about?" I know, obviously, but I'm surprised anyway.

I look down. "What did he say it was about?"

"Stop playing games with me. What's going on?"

"I'm not playing. What did he say?"

"That I need to come in for a conference with all your teachers."

"All of them?"

"That's what he said. Now, what is happening?"

"I owe some work, that's all."

"What does 'some work' mean?"

"I've been distracted; I just have some things to get done. It's not a big deal."

"Don't you lie to me, Sparrow. I've never been called in to school for you before. Don't try to tell me it's not a big deal."

"It's not. I'll get it done."

"Sparrow."

"Yeah?" I say, hanging my head.

"I don't know," she says, and closes the door.

I don't sleep that night. I play the scene through in my head over and over. Faces of my teachers, distorted with my exhaustion, saying over and over, "Sparrow is going to repeat eighth grade" and "Sparrow hasn't done work in months" and "What's *wrong* with your daughter, Ms. Cooke?" Around 2:00 a.m. I go to the window and stare at the empty streets. I open it, just so I can listen for the birds, even though they don't want anything to do with me anymore. I try, but I don't hear anything but a garbage truck and a car alarm, the faraway screeching of wheels down train tracks, the rattle of a bar storefront finally closing. It's not just that birds won't come for me anymore; it's like they've disappeared from the entire city. Like we're all left flightless and I'm the only one awake to notice.

I get out of the house before Mom is out of the shower. I

can't face her. She sends me a text telling me that she'll meet me at school at three. I walk in the door and up the stairs to first period. Kids rush around me, running up the stairs, chatting as they maneuver down them. It all seems effortless, like a beautiful machine. My legs feel like they're made out of iron or lead or whatever's heavier that I'm sure I was supposed to learn at some point this year. I barely get there in time for first period. All morning is like that. My heart pounding in my ears, like I can hear every single blood cell as it swirls around my body. How did this happen? I think back to my colored-in lines, my name on the top of the page, how I used to be shocked when kids wouldn't have their homework. I used to be so good.

I've gone from being my mom's perfect dream child with 100s on her quizzes and the vocabulary of a geek who reads all the time, to a stranger. A bird child with a breakdown. I wish I cared that I'm letting my teachers down. I wish I felt like I was letting myself down. But I don't. I don't care about eighth grade or Mr. Phillips and his thoughts about my "potential." But I care about Mom, and how hard I'm making things for her. I would give anything to go back to the way that it was, being her perfect baby (maybe a little shy, maybe a little strange) with perfect grades, and taking flight when I needed to. She was happier then. So was I.

I didn't do the reading last night. I haven't done homework in two months, it's true, but I always do my reading for Ms. Smith. On my way in, she puts her hand on my shoulder and says, "I'd like to speak with you after class." I spend all period trying to figure out how she knew just from my face that I wasn't prepared. I can't believe I've let her down too. I try to figure out how to get out of this after-class chat. I've seen Jayce do it; he just saunters out with everyone else and ignores the teacher calling his name.

"Can I go to the nurse?" I ask, ten minutes before the end of the period. I go sit in my stall in the bathroom until the bell rings. I go to YouTube on my phone, I put on my headphones and watch the video for "Wolf Like Me" until I hear the rush of people in the hallway. I head out of the stall and literally run into Mr. Garfield.

"Hey, there, Sparrow," he says awkwardly, righting his tie.

"Sorry, Mr. Garfield."

"It's okay. I'm looking forward to meeting your mom later," he says. At that very second, Monique passes by.

"Why are you meeting her mom, Mr. Garfield?" she asks sweetly, and loudly. I notice the gaggle of girls across the hall at their lockers giggling, whispering, admiring her.

"That's none of your business, Monique."

"Sparrow's in trouble? What did you do, little Sparrow? Little Miss Perfect? A parent-teacher conference? Don't worry, Sparrow," she says, throwing her arm around my shoulder, "I'm sure they'll serve Oreos. Unless, wait . . . are they bringing an ambulance? I hear you need those sometimes." I feel everyone's eyes on me now, they're laughing, hooting, Snapchatting.

I throw her arm off me, and storm away from Mr. Garfield's calls of "Sparrow? Are you okay?"

My feet carry me up to the fifth floor. I know at once where my body's headed. I watch my hands unlatch the window that opens farther than it's supposed to; I watch my body bend and ease onto the fire escape. The cold metal feels good on my hands. The roof isn't as cold as it was last time; there's no more snow, just puddles from the last few days of rain, and lots of wind.

The wind blows my hoodie straight back; my eyes water against the heavy gusts. I walk right up to the edge. "Come on!" I say, but they don't come. "Come on!" I shout up to the sky, top of my lungs. "Comeoncomeoncomeon," I'm shouting and sobbing and my lungs hurt and my throat hurts. They're going to leave me here; they left me weeks ago. No one's coming. A strong wind blows behind me, nudging my wet sneakers closer to the ledge. "Get me out of here," I say between sobs, to no one. I feel my toes curl over the edge. I uncurl them. I stop holding on. One more gust, and I'm gone. I can see my body falling through the air. One last flight. I look down and see where my body would fall. I can feel the final swoop of my stomach, the feathers over my arms, my feet tidy underneath me. And I can see the spot on the sidewalk where I would crash into concrete, into dark.

Storm petrels are rare in the city, and if I hadn't spent all my lunch periods since fifth grade in the library, making my way through book after book, I would have thought it was maybe a hawk or a seagull. But no, it's a storm petrel with its wide black wings, soft gray underbelly. Its hard black beak and sweet dark eyes. I'd read once upon a time that storm petrels can appear when it clears after days of rain, but I've never seen one. *Come on*, he says to me. *What are you waiting for? Don't you miss this? Follow me.* And he swoops straight down to the ground. I watch him go, my body folding over my legs, arms dangling in the air below my feet, reaching, dizzy at the height. I can't see him. I imagine my body smashed on the ground at the end of this last flight. I'm not sure that I want to. I'm also not sure that I won't. I can't get myself to back away from the ledge, so I lower my body to the rooftop, inch by inch. I lay my head back, my legs still playing with the air, flirting with flight.

In this daze of death and sky, I hear a bell. I scoot my body backward, away from the edge. I remember the sirens as the ambulance came to get me. I remember the surprised look on the custodian's face when he opened the door to the roof and found me here. I don't want to go back to the hospital, mostly because I don't want to put Mom through that again. I swing my body back down the ladder and through the window and down the hall to class. No one asks where I was. No one is staring at the spot on the sidewalk where my body could have been. Mr. Rothman ushers me into class. I sharpen a pencil. I do a Do Now. Kids around me talk and text and roll their eyes. My body is here. My mind is still on the roof, staring at the empty sky.

The bell rings and from TV on the Radio last night to this moment feels like one hundred years. I sit in Mrs. Robbins's room in a daze, trying to get my feet to stand, to put up my chair, to walk downstairs where Mom will be waiting. Mrs. Robbins turns off the lights. I stand up. "I'll get your chair," she says. Mrs. Robbins never gets anyone's chair. This is going to be just as bad as I think it is.

"Thanks," I say as I head out the door. I put my headphones on and listen to Patti screaming in my ears. Down the hall. Down the stairs. Mom is waiting, black skirt, white blouse, pearls. She is polishing her sunglasses and she stands by the door to the office. She doesn't see me at first. Or maybe she just pretends not to see me.

"Hi," I say. She nods, and takes my headphones off my ears.

Mr. Phillips comes out from the office. "Hi, Ms. Cooke, nice to meet you. I'm Jack Phillips. Come on in." *Swish swish swish.* He leads us to the conference room and points out two chairs for us to sit in. "So, I thought we'd talk for a while, and then you'll have the chance to hear from Sparrow's teachers. How does that sound?"

Mom nods. Under the table, I see that she's picking at her nails. She's not angry (or she's not *just* angry), I realize, she's scared.

"So, we asked you to come in today because obviously this

119

has been a rough year for Sparrow, and she's had a lot of trouble getting her work in."

"Since when?"

"Well, basically . . ." Mr. Phillips is having trouble finishing this sentence. He doesn't want to be rude and mention the hospital.

"Since after I came back, Mom."

He looks at me, grateful. "Yes, exactly. As Sparrow said, it's been hard for her to get work in during these last few months. But I will also say that it's not just limited to homework. Sparrow has a lot of trouble in class too."

"How do you mean?" Mom asks, the edge in her voice teetering over into anger.

"What do I mean, Sparrow?"

"I don't know."

"I think you do. Sparrow has some trouble paying attention in class; it's as if she's somewhere else most of the time. Between that and her homework, her grades have taken a real dip this semester."

"I see."

"I'd like to bring in a few of her teachers to talk more specifically about what she owes and how she can turn this around. There's still time, Sparrow." Of course there's time, what there's not is a different me.

One by one, Mrs. Robbins, Mr. Rothman, and Mr. Garfield all come in. They all say the same thing: I'm checked out, I owe work, I need to get every assignment in for the rest of the year or I won't pass, and there's the small matter of my participation. There's a chorus of *You're such a smart girl* and *You can turn it around* and *Don't you want to go to high school?* Mom nudges me in the ribs and I sit up and nod, I make promises, I make eye contact. Part of me even believes that I'll go home and do my homework tonight.

Mr. Phillips bring this funfest to an end, telling me that I can do it, telling Mom to call if anything comes up. He shakes her hand, *swish swish swishing* out the door, and leaving me alone with Mom.

"I'm sorry," I say. She's silent. She reaches for her bag, and pushes back her chair as Ms. Smith comes in. I want to disappear. I hate that I've disappointed her too.

"It's so nice to meet you, Ms. Cooke," she says, extending her hand. Mom takes it, and manages a smile. "Sparrow is an extraordinary girl." Mom is stiffening, preparing for the *but*. She tries to look at me, but I've been counting the black flecks in the carpet for what feels like hours now.

"I know it's been hard for her, but she's been great in English. Her writing is gorgeous and funny and detailed. She's a tremendous reader." I lose count of the black flecks. "She's creative and talented, and while I know she's gotten into some hot water this year, I wanted to come by and say that in my class, that's simply not the case."

I sneak a quick glance at Mom. She swallows hard, and then smiles. "Thank you," she says. "I know how much she loves your class."

"Well, I love having her. Now, Sparrow, I know that you need some extra credit." I nod. She clears her throat. She's waiting for me to look at her. I force my head up; it weighs a million pounds, but I do it. "I know you know that I'm in charge of the talent show this year."

"Ms. Smith, I appreciate the offer, but I'm not going to —"

"Sparrow, you are not in a position to negotiate. You are going to listen to what Ms. Smith has to say." It's the first sentence Mom has said to me since last night.

"Sorry," I say.

"Don't worry, Sparrow, I'm not going to ask you to perform, I'm not that much of a monster." She smiles and her cheeks push her black-rimmed glasses up.

I look at her, and I smile too. "What, then?"

"I want you to run tech for the talent show. I would have told you after class if you hadn't ducked out to the nurse. You're going to learn how to run the light board; you're going to help me order the performances and rehearse them and make sure that everything goes smoothly. What do you think?"

"I don't have to sing or dance or a read a sonnet or whatever?"

"No."

"She'd love to."

"I'd love to."

"Okay."

"Thank you," I stammer.

"Thank you," says Mom, and we all file out. Ms. Smith goes up the stairs to her classroom and we head out into the evening for the silent walk home. Mom doesn't speak until we're finally sitting at the island in the kitchen. Mom is a slow burn; she's not going to let it all out at once. She holds tight to her feelings until they're boiling over. She likes to be inside when that happens.

"Just say it, Mom," I say as I rock my feet back and forth on the stool.

"Say what, Sparrow?"

"Just tell me how mad you are at me, what a failure I am, how this isn't how you raised me, how disappointed you are."

"Why? Why bother, Sparrow? You're going to do what you're going to do anyway, and it seems like it's been quite a while since you've listened to what I've had to say."

"It's not that."

"It is that. I'll tell you what else it is. You can shut me out all you like, little girl, that's fine. But you're not going to screw up your future so you can sit in your bedroom and play air guitar. Starting Monday, you're coming to the office every day after school and you'll sit with James and you'll work until I'm ready to come home." James is Mom's assistant at the bank.

"I have therapy on Monday."

"About that. I can't really see how it's helping you."

"It's helping."

"Not as far as I can tell. As far as I can tell, you're not paying attention at school, you're not talking to me, you spend all your time in your room or staring off to who knows what in the backyard, you still won't tell me what happened, you still won't tell me anything, and now for the first time in your life, you're failing school? *Failing*, Sparrow. And you're telling me that therapy is helping?"

I stare at the ground. I feel like I've spent all day this way.

"Look at me when I'm talking to you, Sparrow." I look up. I look her straight in the face, which is not the best idea. She'll take it as defiance, which I guess it is.

"It's helping, Mom. I'm sorry you can't see it, I'm sorry you don't like Dr. Katz. I'm sorry you don't like that I'm listening to angry music all the time. And I am really, really sorry that school is such a mess and that I've screwed up so bad. I get that this is a big deal. But the solution isn't taking me out of therapy; it's the only thing that helps. You think this is bad? This is nothing."

"This is nothing?"

"I can't talk about this anymore." I get up and go upstairs, knowing that this is the last thing that I should do. She appears in my doorway one minute later.

"You can't walk away from me, Sparrow."

"I'm sorry."

"Things have got to change around here. I've let you be too independent. You want to go to therapy so bad? That woman means that much to you? Fine. But every other day you will be at my office after school, working. Is that clear?"

"Yes."

"Good night." She shuts off my light and closes the door. I'm fully dressed and wide-awake and it's one of those moments when you just know that things are going to get worse.

And they do. Kind of. I'm scared enough of Mom, and of disappointing her more, that I manage to stay awake in most of my classes for the rest of the week. I go to her office and sit with James after school. James is a nice guy; he's young and new, just as scared of Mom as I am. I sit on the couch outside her office and watch YouTube videos on my phone. He offers me a snack from the candy drawer that he keeps in his desk. I take some peanut butter cups and stare off some more.

"Where's Mom?" I ask him, one headphone still on my ear.

"Meetings for the rest of the day, kiddo," he says. So, I don't have to worry that she'll come by to check on me with her neutral face, which is just a cover for her angry face. I don't have to worry about whether she is more or less angry than she was the day before. And I don't have to worry about that silence, that heavy, lasting silence that has been following us around since long before she left me in my room with the lights off. I put both headphones on and unwrap the candy. After a few minutes, James is kneeling in front of me.

"What are you listening to?"

"TV on the Radio."

"They're dope," he says. I smile and nod, not taking off my headphones. He reaches up and grabs one off of my ear. "Listen, kid. I don't know if you know this, but your mom is pretty scary."

"I've noticed."

"So, if she comes back here and you're eating candy and rocking out, we're going to have a serious problem."

"I know."

"And I'm not talking about you and your mom, I'm talking about your mom and me. I can't have her angry at me, short stuff. That's just not going to work. So, whatever it is that you're supposed to work on, can you at least look like you're working on it?"

"Yeah, okay."

"What are you supposed to be working on?" I hold up my entire backpack with its three packets of makeup work and all of tonight's assignments. He tries to lift it and then fake falls under its weight. "You better get going, then."

16

Sometimes I wake up around four thirty, when the sun is just starting to come up and my neighborhood is this weird pink that doesn't seem to fit the city streets and building-block houses or the traffic, and I look out the window and want with everything I've got to be up in the air just one more time. I'm not trying to fly away from anything, I'm really not, but when you spend your whole life wrapped in blue, wind at your back, sun-soaked and soaring, it's hard to settle for just walking around. It's hard to settle for the subway and school and watching TV.

I go to school and work on those endless packets while everyone is talking to each other, and then I go to the office and eat candy with James and do work and wait for Mom and then go home with her on what always seems like an eerily quiet subway car and then avoid her and listen to music in my room until I fall asleep. It's fine; it's better than a hospital, but it's not like my life was. It's not like I can't tell that something is missing. I don't know how everyone does it, walking around in bodies that are nothing other than what they are. Being themselves and never anyone, or any*thing*, else. I guess it's okay to wander around without the *swoop swoop* of your heart rising and falling in your chest and your wings stretching over water if you've never had it.

I sit at the island and eat my cereal, and it's like I can't even get myself to bring the spoon to my mouth because what's the point? The cereal looks like twigs in my milk; it reminds me a little of a nest. Great.

"Bye, Mom!" I call as I leave. She's running late today, or maybe she's started going to work later so that she can avoid me in the mornings. It's fine. I walk to school and let the crowd push me along to my first-period class. I don't have to think about it; I just follow the swarm. When I get to my classroom, I stand on line and read *The Perks of Being a Wallflower* and wait—wait to get into class, wait for the day to end.

In English, we're starting to read *The Great Gatsby*, which I only like because Charlie's also reading it in *The Perks of Being a Wallflower*. The popular girls ask if we can see the movie. Ms. Smith says absolutely not, and that's why I like Ms. Smith. I never like movies that books get turned into. She asks me to help pass out books, which I don't like because I feel the other kids watch me as I walk around the room, but I think she's just testing me to make sure I'm ready to be her assistant, so I do it. Also, it's not like she's actually giving me a choice. When I get back to my seat, there's a note on top of *Perks*. It says *Charlie is the best. Do you like the Bots?* I look around my table, and everyone seems completely fascinated as Ms.

Smith introduces the book, telling us about Fitzgerald's life and asking us for a definition of materialism. Nobody seems like they've just finished writing a secret note to someone they've never spoken to. But then again, what would that look like?

Everyone is trying to start to pack up without Ms. Smith noticing—she doesn't like it when you pack up before the bell. I try to think of who might have left me a note. I've never gotten one before. I look around my table at the five other kids I've been sitting with since September. Are any of them secret indie rock fans? Not Christina, who's best friends with Monique. Not Zahara, who wears pink shirts with rhinestones and loves, loves, loves Katy Perry. Noah sometimes rides a skateboard, so maybe, but why would he write me a note? The truth about Tanasia is that I don't know anything about her. She sits with the second-tier popular kids at lunch, she seems nice, but does she blast indie rock in her spare time? I just don't know. It's nice to feel something in my stomach besides dread—what is it? Curiosity? There's the tiniest spring in my step as I slip the note into my pocket and head to the door.

On my way out of the classroom, Ms. Smith stops me to say that rehearsals will begin next week, just us at first so I can "learn the ropes." I'll need to be in the theater from three to five on Tuesdays and Thursdays. I say okay, what else can I say? My heart sinks to my feet as I realize this means talking to Mom about not coming to the office, which means she'll have to trust me to not fail out of school, and that doesn't seem likely.

When I get home from the office that night, I rush through the door and upstairs to my room. I start to download the Bots. I click related artists over and over; I add Thunderbitch, Courtney Barnett, Benjamin Booker, and Tune-Yards. My feet kick against the floor in time. I watch video after video. I can't take my eyes off the hands of the bass players. My packet of worksheets, my impending academic doom, the hospital, Dr. Katz, even Mom, it's not that they feel far away; it's that they feel like a foreign language, an alien planet. Nothing to do with me and this good noise. I didn't know you could feel this free with both feet on the ground.

"Sparrow? Come on in."

"Hi." I have a seat and see what we've got going on today. I guess Dr. K is feeling funky, rocking her yellow-and-green Roos and a yellow-and-red shirt that I think is what batik means and a leather vest. With fringe.

"Hi." She says the word like it has a few extra *iii*'s at the end, like she's waiting for me. "So, how's it been on the ground?"

"Kind of boring, honestly. Everything is okay, except for feeling like something is missing all the time. Like part of me is . . . not dead, maybe, but dying? It's like when you have a scab and you can't stop picking at it and it turns into a scar and then you pick at that, even though it's just skin, but it feels like a different kind of skin, like a stump? Does any of this make any sense?"

"Yep." She smiles. "I want to talk about something from last time. Why the roof?" I think about my most recent visit up there and shudder a little inside. I know I should tell her. I will. I will.

"It's such a boring answer. I wasn't up there for any special reason, okay? I was up there because that's where I go. After that terrible week with Monique and Leticia, I realized that most people don't actually notice if I'm missing, so instead of going to lunch I'd go to the roof, because the cafeteria sucked and the roof is quiet and empty and a lot of birds come by."

"Why do you think it's been so hard for you to answer that question?"

"It's the only thing anyone wants to know, why I was on that roof, and the answer is so simple, but I couldn't tell them because how do you explain to everyone that you have no friends and lunch is hell and so you go up to the roof to hang out with the birds because they like you and are nice to you, and oh, by the way, you also happen to turn into one from time to time?"

"Who's everyone?"

"Everyone who's asked me about going to the roof."

"Who's that?"

"Well, you a million times, to start with."

"Yep, but even after you told me about flying, you couldn't tell me about the roof. Why not?"

"It just became this *thing*, like, ooooh, why was she on the roof, and with everyone else I can't answer the question because I can't tell them that I was flying, and with you I couldn't answer it because I'd been refusing to answer it for so long."

"How does it feel now that you've told me?"

"Anticlimactic."

"Ha. Who else has asked you?"

"The doctors."

"Who else?"

"No one, really." Except Mom, I think. Her name brings tiny stabbing pinpricks at the back of my eyes. I'm not in the mood.

"Sparrow."

"What?"

She's going to insist, I can tell. I can tell, this is what the next eighteen minutes are going to be about. I can wait it out.

"Sparrow."

"What?" I snap this time. "I'm done."

"You're not, really."

"I have seventeen minutes and thirty seconds left and I'm done."

"You'll be done in seventeen minutes and thirty seconds."

"Twenty-nine."

"In the meantime, I asked you a question."

"Yeah, and I answered it. Sorry you don't like my answer." These days I seem to be setting a record for being rude to adults. I mean, I know I've gotten angry at Dr. Katz before, but this feels different. I used to get angry and help myself out the window. Now I'm angry and I'm here, and my hands are fists and my face is hot.

"You can be angry at me, Sparrow, that's fine. . . ." I hear her say in the background. I don't hear the rest. I do not feel my body doing it, but I know it's happening. Suddenly I am standing. Suddenly I'm at the door. Suddenly I'm gone.

I run down the beige-white-green hallway to the door at the end and take the stairs two at a time until I'm at the street and people are walking by me like it's just a regular day. They're coming home from work or picking up their kids or getting out of a taxi or going grocery shopping. I run across the street and head up, up, up the hill. My legs know where I'm going even when I don't, like at school when I tell myself I won't eat lunch in the bathroom today and end up there anyway. I'm running up the hill, and though I've done it many times, I'm still surprised to find myself at the park and out of breath.

I keep going deeper into the park, past the soccer fields and the dog beach and the baseball diamonds and the people riding horses in the middle of the afternoon, to the lake my mom used to take me to when I was little. I guess it's technically a pond, but it's got swans and geese and it reflects the blue sky and the big puffs of white clouds. I wipe my eyes with the back of my hand and pick up some rocks. I see Dr. Katz's face in the water and throw the rocks at it over and over again. I like watching her disappear. I watch the swans until they start spreading their wings and my heart goes heavy inside my chest. I walk back through the soccer fields and hide out in the shade of the trees, watching the boys playing soccer with their dads and wishing they'd kick hard and fast at my head instead.

I stay a long time, longer than I should. I watch the sun go down over the soccer fields; the dads toss their kids on their shoulders and carry them home. Finally, one of those pretend cops comes by in his little golf cart and tells me to head home. For a while, I think about just sleeping here, like the kids in *From the Mixed-Up Files of Mrs. Basil E. Frankweiler*. Look it up. It's a book. Mrs. Wexler gave it to me and I love it. It's about these two kids who sneak into the Metropolitan Museum of Art and stay there. I remember thinking they were so brave. And that it sounded like such a good backup plan. Every time a teacher would drag our class to the Met for a field trip, I'd look around for good hiding spots, but I knew I would never be able to do anything that brave. I was right—I'm not that brave. I consider the park bench for a minute, but mostly I think about the different kinds of animals and humans that go through the park at night, and I decide to head home.

It starts to rain suddenly, the way it does sometimes in the spring—kind of warm until it's dark and cold and not warm at all anymore. I walk another twenty blocks home down the hill and across the neighborhood, soaked through my sneakers, my hoodie, my hair. Alone and a mess.

Some kids have curfews, or at least they do in TV shows. I don't have a curfew. I've never come home late in my life. I've never had anywhere to come home from. So, I wasn't breaking a rule, technically. Well, I guess I did break one. I'm supposed to pick up the phone whenever my mom calls, no matter what. She called three times while I was at the park. I look at my phone and consider calling her back, but I just keep walking. When I get home, I am expecting her to be pacing the floor arms crossed, steam coming out of her ears. I am expecting to hear it all night long from her, to hear about how I scared her half to death, what in the world was I thinking, don't I know better, didn't she raise me not to do foolish things like this, go to your room, I can't even talk to you right now, and on and on.

But my mother isn't at the door. She's at the island, eyes red. Even though I've never seen her do it before, I know she's been crying. She's wearing her bathrobe, hand around a cup of tea that went cold a long time ago. When I walk in, I hear her say, "Oh, thank God." That's all she says. She doesn't ask where I've been. She doesn't call me a fool. She doesn't send me to my room or threaten to ground me until I go to college. She doesn't even look at me as I cross the kitchen to go to the bathroom and hang up my wet things. I'm hanging my jeans on the hook on the back of the door when she says, "I know you want me to say something, Sparrow, but I swear to God I have no idea what to say to you anymore." Her voice cracks while she says it, like more tears would come if only she had them. Then I hear her put her cup in the sink, go up the stairs to her room, and close the door. I sleep on the mat on the floor of the bathroom. I can't bear the idea of running into her. I'm also pretty sure that a person who makes her mother cry like that doesn't deserve a bed.

17

The bathroom at school stops being a bathroom when I start watching YouTube videos there during lunch. It starts with the Bots, and then I just let the YouTube gods take me where they will, skipping anything that doesn't reach that spot right between my heart and my ribs. At first, the song title just makes me laugh; "Shithole" seems pretty appropriate for my current setting. But that's not what makes me stay. It's that my feet can't sit still. It's that she says "hoping for something to take me off this land," and I think she might understand. It's that with her blond curls, light skin, and crazy, fluorescent dress she looks like she could be Dr. K's daughter. Or that if Dr. K was twenty-five now, this is who she would be. Thinking of Katz doesn't even bring me down. I'm lost in the bass line, in the lyrics, in my sneakers beating against the stall door and not caring who hears. I download every Weaves song I can find. If I ever figure out who wrote me that note, maybe I'll tell her (him?) about them. If I ever speak to Katz again, maybe I'll tell her.

"Come on in." I sit down in my seat and stare at everything but her for a long time. I can't believe it was just a week ago that I ran out of here.

"I'm sorry," I mumble.

Dr. Katz peers down too, trying to catch my eye and raise it to meet hers. "You don't need to apologize to me, Sparrow. It's your session, you can do whatever you like with it, including leave."

"Oh."

"So, where'd you go?"

"To the park."

"Watch the birds?"

"Not really. I went to the pond I used to go to with my mom when I was a kid."

"Ah. You live in North Slope, right?"

"Yeah."

"That's pretty far from home. When did you get home?"

I'm a goner. I know where this is going. I might as well give up right now. Before the sentence is even out of my mouth, tears are all over my face. I wipe them off with my hoodie. This particular hoodie has been through a lot in the last week.

"I got home late."

"Was your mom worried?"

Answering her hurts too much. I double over like I have a stomachache. It feels better, my face against my knees, my arms around my middle. Like a hug. I realize how long it's been since I've had a hug from anyone, and the sobs come stronger. Finally, I get up and go over to her iPod dock. I put mine in.

It's the song I was playing over and over again in my headphones after I left last week. I watch Dr. Katz's face as I sit down. I have a pretty decent vocabulary for someone my age, but I don't know the word for the look on her face. Like maybe she's listened to this song on a park bench while throwing rocks into water?

"Do you know it?" I ask, wiping my snotty nose.

"Elliott Smith."

"Yeah."

"It's a beautiful song."

I nod.

He starts on the second verse. This music is a lot softer than what I usually listen to, but he can do it too — reach the deep-down parts, speak them out loud even though you were certain you were the only person who had those particular parts.

"Somebody that you used to know?"

I don't know how she knows. I nod. It's all I can do.

"You feel that way about your mom?"

"She feels that way about me," I squeak out.

"Did you tell her where you'd been?"

"She didn't ask."

"How did that make you feel?"

"Like she doesn't care about me anymore. But I don't think that's it; I think I've convinced her that there's nothing her caring will do. So she can care about me but it doesn't matter, and she's exhausted. Too tired to care about me now; I've worn her out."

We sit for a second and let the song finish out.

"I went back to the roof," I say. She nods. She looks at me, maybe sadly. "Things have been bad at school."

"What happened?"

"I haven't been able to do work, so I might have to repeat eighth grade if I can't get my grades up, which means that every day I'm not here after school, I'm at my mom's office doing homework. But what it meant first was a huge fight with Mom when she found out. And then it meant a parent-teacher conference at school that Monique found out about."

"Yikes."

"Yeah. I've just never felt like I've let that many people down before. Mom was so upset, and Monique was bitchy Monique and I . . . I didn't know where else to go."

"So you went to the roof."

"Yeah. But it didn't feel like it did before."

"Because you can't fly anymore?"

I nod. I swallow hard. I try to get her to read my thoughts so I don't have to say them. I pull my hands into the sleeves of my hoodie.

"What were you thinking about while you were up there?"

"About flying. Without the birds."

"That sounds more like jumping." I hang my head. If she can tell that's a nod, good for her.

"Okay. What kept you from doing it?" I notice that she's not secretly dialing 911. She doesn't sound panicked. She's just asking me more Katz-y questions, the way she always does.

"I don't know. Mom, I guess. I don't think I wanted to be dead as much as I wanted to be gone."

"You're pretty used to being gone."

"Yeah. And I can't anymore. And sometimes that sucks. Maybe I'm just stubborn, and I didn't want them to be right."

"Who?"

"The people who think I tried to kill myself." I take a deep breath. "Mom."

"What have you told her?"

"Nothing."

"Literally?"

"Pretty much. I miss her," I say quietly, to myself mostly.

"I bet." Dr. Katz lets me sit there, just sit there missing her. "Sparrow, I'm going to say something that's going to make you want to leave the room. You can if you have to, but I want you to try to stay."

"Okay."

"Do you think you can tell your mom what happened?"

"No."

"Do you want to?"

I don't know how to answer. Kind of? Hell no? You first?

She's not even speaking to me right now and I'm going to be like, *Mom, you can stop worrying, I'm fine, I just turn into a bird every once in a while, I'm working it out in therapy, nbd.*

"I don't know."

"Well, why haven't you told her?"

"I don't want her to feel bad. Who wants a kid who's crazy?"

"You're crazy? I hadn't noticed."

"I'm not normal."

"Do you think your mother thinks you're normal?"

"I think she'd like it if I could at least pretend to be. I think she wants me to be like her. And that would mean not turning into a bird, not going to the hospital, not being in therapy at fourteen."

"Has she said that you shouldn't be in therapy?"

"She says she doesn't think it's helping. But, I guess, what would she know? It's not like I talk to her about it. Or anything."

"You'll never know if you don't give her the chance."

"Ugh."

"Yeah, ugh. But still, the question is, do you like how things are going with your mom or do you want to try something else?"

"I don't want to be somebody she used to know."

"Right."

"I can't tell her. I just won't. I know I won't."

"Why don't we tell her together?"

"I think I just threw up in my mouth a little."

She laughs. "That's disgusting, but I take your point. Still, it might be a little easier to bring your mom in. That way, at least I can help you understand each other. Maybe you'll be able to start talking to her, even if it's just a little."

"Whatever. Okay. It's not like it's going to make it worse."

"That's the spirit. Ask her to come next week."

On the way out the door, I say, "Do you know Weaves? I think you might like them."

18

I told Mom that I needed to do rehearsal for the talent show instead of coming to her office. It went like this:

Me: Mom, I can't come to the office today. I have to go to rehearsal for the talent show with Ms. Smith.

Mom: (Silent.)

Me: So, can I?

Mom: I want to see all your work before you go to bed.

Me: Okay.

Mom: (Nods. Leaves the room.)

This completely fantastic interaction has not left me a lot of hope for the conversation in which I ask her to come to therapy with me. I try to psych myself up, to get myself to ask her. Instead, I just look like a creeper. I go into her room; she's in her bathroom doing her makeup. I stand there telling myself that when she comes out, I'm going to ask her to come to therapy with me. When I hear her put down her lipstick, I run out of the room. "Sparrow?" she calls. I don't answer. I sit at the island, poking at my cereal and promising myself that when she comes downstairs, I'll say it. I hear the creak of the stairs as she starts down them, and I literally run out of the house. I don't even say good-bye.

"Sparrow." It's Tanasia whispering to me. I don't think I've ever heard her voice before.

"What?"

"Your turn." I look up and the whole class is looking at me, including Ms. Smith over her glasses, which is never a good sign.

"You weren't paying attention," says Ms. Smith.

"Right. Sorry."

" 'Sorry' is for when you're not going to do it again."

I have heard Ms. Smith say this a million times, but never to me. I want to fall through the floor. I keep my face very still so that I don't cry.

"So, can you tell me what you think about the relationship between Nick and Gatsby?"

"He idolizes him."

"Yes, we have that already." She gestures to the board, where the class has apparently been making a list for quite a while. "Does anyone else have anything new?"

With her eyes off me, I can start to breathe again. Tanasia sneaks me a smile, like it happens to everyone. Except that it never happens to me, at least not in English. At the end of the period, I still want to fall through the floor and I'm trying to get out of the room as fast as I can.

"Sparrow." Ms. Smith stops me.

I sigh. "Yes?" I look up because I don't want her to say what adults always say when you don't want to look at them: *Look at me when I'm talking to you!*

"Tough day. See you at the theater at three."

"Okay." She doesn't seem mad, but it'll be a while before my stomach untwists.

⤙

When I get to the theater at three, Ms. Smith is already there. "Hi!" she says happily from the stage. "Come on down, I promise I won't make you sing and dance." I head to the front and take a seat near her.

"That's the light booth up there; we'll get there last. First you're going to get to know backstage. That's where I'll be. The night of the show, you're going to be in the light booth, but before that you'll be backstage with me making sure all the props are where they should be and everyone knows the set order. Okay? Good. Come," she says, and we sneak behind the heavy green curtain.

Backstage looks like a construction site, all beams and hidden walkways. It smells warm and slightly dusty. There's a table that Ms. Smith says will be the prop table; she tells me I'll collect props from everyone and put them on the table in order of how they'll be used by each performer. She tells me we'll have walkie-talkies so that she'll be able to communicate with me in the light booth if anything needs to be adjusted—because, she says casually, I'll also be running sound.

"Isn't that kind of a lot? I don't know how to do any of this."

"True, you would have learned in a performing arts class if you'd taken one. Pity."

I open my mouth to protest but she says, smiling, "It's okay, Sparrow. You're a quick learner and we have two weeks before the performance."

As we head up to the light booth, I say, "I really am sorry about class today."

"Well, I know you wish it hadn't happened, but, my dear, it's not the first time. You're almost always just on your way back from somewhere else."

"What do you mean?"

"You know what I mean. You're here, but you're also far away."

"I'm trying to be here more."

"I know that too. It's okay. It's hard to be here sometimes."

I feel my face getting warm, but not because I'm embarrassed.

"Let's take a look at this."

Ms. Smith shows me the light board and she lets me play

around with the settings. I make the theater really bright, and then I make a really narrow spotlight, I make everything bright blue, I make it orange. She laughs.

"Okay, but mostly you're going to use this one." She shows me how to make a spotlight in the middle of the stage.

"That's it?"

"That's it. Now let's take a look at sound." She stands onstage with a microphone (reading selections from *Gatsby*, of course), and I practice getting the levels right until it's time to go home.

"That's a wrap!" calls Ms. Smith as she heads toward the light booth.

"Thanks for letting me do this," I say.

"You're most welcome. It seemed like it was even—let me see if I can find the right word—fun?"

I smile. "Maybe."

"That's a good start. I'll see you tomorrow."

"I'll be there." I mean it in every sense.

She's right. It was fun. So much fun that for the last hour or more, I haven't thought about what's waiting for me at home. My feet move more and more slowly as I get close to the house. I wait on the steps for Mom. She'll be home any minute now. I sit and read my *Gatsby* assignment, and a piece of paper falls out of the book. A small square in the same handwriting as the last one. It just says *They say I'm different*. . . . My heart skips a beat. Either they're making fun of me or this is a clue of some kind. I want to go google it right now but I feel Mom turn the corner onto the block. So that I don't just sit and stare at her until she turns into our gate, I keep my eyes on the page, rereading the same sentence over and over, sticking the note in the back of the book. The words aren't even making sense anymore; it's just a place to keep my eyes until I can look up. I hear the gate creak.

"Hi, Mom."

"How was rehearsal?"

"Good. I know I've got to work to do; I'll try to get it done."

"Coming in?"

"Sure. There's, um, there's kind of something I want to talk to you about." No turning back now.

"Okay." I follow her into the living room and she sits on the couch. This seems like a good sign. Like what a happy family on TV might do to have a Big Talk.

"So, um, obviously, I've had some, um, trouble talking."

"Right." She seems nervous. Who can blame her? I sound like a lunatic.

"Dr. Katz . . ." I can't finish the sentence.

"We can find you someone else if you want. Or maybe you're done?" It's impossible not to hear the hope in her voice. Things are looking less sitcom every second.

"Um, no, it's not that. It's fine with her. It's, um, it's good. She wanted me to ask you to come to the next session. With me. Can you?"

"Of course."

"Cool. Thanks."

"You don't have to thank me, Sparrow; I'm your mother. If you want me to come, I'll be there."

"I want you to."

"That's that, then."

Okay. It's done. I let out all the breath I've been holding for days. We're not cuddling, but it's possible I'll be speaking with her earlier than college. Mostly all I can think is *it's done it's done it's done.*

"Do you want to order Indian?" she asks.

"Yes, definitely, yes."

"The usual?"

"Sure." I turn on the TV. It's the doctor show she loves. "Want to watch?" I ask, hoping she'll let us watch and eat.

"Sure," she says. "Get your backpack. You can get at least three math problems done during the commercials."

After Indian food, an episode of the doctor show, and a full sheet of math plus homework for tonight, Mom releases me to my room. I sit at my computer and type in the words. The first result is the one I'm meant to see. Betty Davis roars into my stereo. I play what is so clearly meant to be the loudest song on earth quiet enough for Mom not to come storming into my room; I wouldn't try to contain this voice in headphones. I fall asleep with the slightest smile on my face.

19

We wait in the waiting room. *We.* The word makes my skin crawl. Just like at my first session, we sit there, not speaking. I'm staring up at the very familiar ceiling, my mom is riffling through the same six magazines that have been here since at least February. My heart is beating out of my chest. What was I thinking? What was Dr. Katz thinking? I'll just tell my mother, and poof, everything will be fine? We'll be wrapped in pink fairy dust and ride away into the sunset together, mother and child reunited at last? Yeah, right, lady.

"Hi, Sparrow, Ms. Cooke. Come on in."

I hate this already. I can't sit in my chair because we have to sit on the sofa by the wall. This throws everything off. We sit on opposite ends. My mother crosses her legs and keeps her folded hands in her lap. This is formal Mom; this is Mom in a business meeting, her favorite self. She's just come from work, still in her suit and pearls.

Let's see what this woman thinks she can tell me about my daughter, I can hear her thinking.

"Thank you for coming, Ms. Cooke," says Dr. Katz.

"Of course," she says, as if there's nowhere else she'd rather be. Dr. Katz might not be able to see through it, but I can.

"How has Sparrow seemed at home?"

"She seems quiet." Mom is pleasant, but not giving an inch.

"More than usual?"

"More than usual with me, yes."

"Well, I think that's why Sparrow wanted you to come here today." Dr. Katz looks at me. This is a question disguised as a sentence. She's waiting for me to answer. Mom is looking at me too, like a stopwatch. *Come on already.*

"Yeah. Sometimes it's like, I haven't said anything for such a long time that it just gets too hard to start."

"You can always talk to me, Sparrow. You didn't need to bring me here to talk to me." Instead, I look down, the pit in my stomach growing by the second. I can feel her shift on the couch, her ankles crossed.

"I know. I'm sorry."

"Why are you sorry, Sparrow?" asks Dr. Katz.

"I'm sorry that I dragged her out of work."

"Talk to your mom directly."

"I'm sorry that I dragged you out of work." My stomach feels queasy. I think about what would happen if I just threw up right here on the rug. That would bring an end to this real quick.

"It's okay, Sparrow. I don't mind missing work. I just mean that if you want to talk to me, all you have to do is talk."

"I know, but it got too hard to just start."

"Well, I'm glad you started." Mom sounds like she's all set, ready to leave. I almost feel her get up from the couch. *Problem solved. Sparrow's talking again. Thanks for all your hard work, Doc.*

You wish, Mom. We're just getting going.

"Sparrow, why do you think it's been so hard for you to talk to your mom?"

"I feel embarrassed."

"Why would you feel embarrassed?" Mom asks, shocked. Her eyes wide, her eyebrows reaching for her hairline. Her weight is settling down into the gray cushions. Defeated.

"Mom, come on, a kid in the mental hospital at fourteen, barely passing eighth grade—that's not really what you had in mind, is it?" Mom looks at me and she looks just like Mom. Not like the last-three-and-a-half-months Mom. Like actual Mom. She'll be back to her business self in a second, I'm sure, but it's nice to see that I haven't destroyed Old Mom.

"Sparrow, the person you are is exactly the person I had in mind." Mom plans meals weeks ahead; she irons the shirt she needs next Tuesday last Wednesday. She has been telling me since I was six years old that I need to sit up straight, talk more, make friends, do something with my hair. Mom has very specific things in mind, and a bird-daughter with terrible shyness and a dirty hoodie was never one of them. My hands grow clammy and my cheeks are hot, but I make myself say it anyway.

"It doesn't seem that way. I feel like . . . I've always felt like you'd rather I be . . . easier. Someone who has friends and goes to parties and cares about her hair and doesn't hide under the coats on the first day of school. Someone who doesn't care about what other people think of her, who's confident and friendly and *NORMAL*. Someone more like you."

"Oh, Sparrow." Mom's voice breaks just a little as she inhales. She grips her hands tighter, but not like she's angry. Like she's trying to keep them still. "Baby, if I tried to push you to talk to people, to have friends, to be more social, it's not because I wanted *you* to be easier but because I wanted your life to be easier."

"Easier than what?" you-know-who asks.

Mom cuts her eyes just slightly at Dr. Katz. She does not take well to being questioned by strangers, certainly not by ones who think they know her daughter better than she does.

"Well," Mom begins, her voice even, cold to the touch, "Sparrow knows what I mean."

"Do you?" Dr. Katz asks.

"I guess," I say, looking down.

Mom looks at me. She draws in a breath, and I can feel her softening against her will. Her shoulders lean just slightly toward the back of the couch.

"Sparrow, who's my best friend?"

"Aunt Joan."

"That's right. My twin sister. When we were in school, I couldn't bear to talk to anyone. Joanie made all the friends. Mostly, they put up with me because that was the cost of being

Joan's friend—you had to be my friend too. Do you know what I did on the first day of school when I was little? I ran home. I hid in my closet for the rest of the day. My parents switched me into Joanie's class after that. They didn't know what else to do, and they couldn't keep leaving work every time I ran away from school."

"That's just like me. Why didn't you tell me?" I'm still looking down, but Mom's hand has moved from her own grip to the pillow between us on the couch, like she's reaching for me.

"I was terrified when you were the same way. You didn't have a Joanie; who was going to look out for you the way Joanie did for me?"

"What about you?" I ask, trying to keep the accusation out of my voice.

"What about me, baby? I have the same problem you do, and I couldn't send Aunt Joan with you to school. So I tried to get you to toughen up, to get past it the way I never had. I came down so hard on you because I didn't want it to be as bad for you as it had been for me."

Whenever I tried to imagine my mother at my age before, she looked exactly like herself, just shorter, more flat-chested, still wearing a suit and pearls, holding a briefcase, hair perfect, shirt starched. Suddenly the camera in my mind zooms out and I can see that she's just a skinny girl standing alone, not so different from someone else I know. I stare at her like I'm seeing her for the first time, which I guess I am.

"I just figured that was something wrong with me and I didn't have whatever I needed to fix it." We sit in silence for a minute. I can feel the muscles in her jaw tighten. She swallows.

"Is that why you tried to kill yourself?" Finally. The words fly out of her mouth like they've been sitting there for months trying to push their way past her teeth.

"Mom."

"Am I not allowed to ask?"

"No, it's not that." Can I do it? Can I say what it is?

Dr. Katz is looking at me. *This is why we're here*, she seems to be telling me, *you can swim or you can drown.*

"Mom, I wasn't trying to kill myself."

"You say that, Sparrow, and I appreciate that you don't want me to worry or to feel bad, but I know what happened. I know what I saw."

"What happened?" asks Dr. Katz.

"They called me to the hospital because Sparrow had been found trying to jump off the roof of her school. When I got there, they had sedated her because she'd been hysterical. I only got to take her home on the condition that she see you. Since then, her denial has been so thick, all she'll say is that she didn't try to kill herself. I don't know what else you would call it."

"Sparrow, what do you call it?"

Mom is facing me again. So is Dr. Katz. What do I call it?

"I call it flying." I thought maybe I would feel relief. But

155

what it feels like instead is that the dual boulders that rest on top of my shoulders have lodged themselves in the middle of my throat instead. I wait for Mom to pick me up and carry me to the mental hospital herself. I wait for the floor to open and swallow me whole. I wait for the world to stop spinning. Instead, all that happens is that Mom finally says, "You think you can fly?"

"I *can* fly. Or at least I could."

"Ms. Cooke, under a lot of emotional stress, Sparrow tends to check out from whatever situation she's in. She might physically be in one place, but mentally she's pretty far away."

"She's flying?" Mom asks incredulously.

"For her, yes, she is. Is she literally, physically growing wings and soaring? Not that we would notice. But for her? Absolutely."

"She thinks I'm crazy," I say.

"Talk to your mother directly," says Dr. K.

"You think I'm crazy."

She's quiet for a few seconds that feel like years. She's looking at the ceiling, trying to read it for the answer.

"I'm thinking that's what you were doing on the porch. Honestly, Sparrow, I don't know. Is this normal? What does this mean for her?"

"What are you afraid it means?" Dr. Katz asks.

"Hospitals, medications, never being able to lead a regular life." Mom looks down, ceiling to floor, the same dance I've done a million times in this room.

"I don't think we have to worry about those things with Sparrow if she continues learning how to confront the issues that make her feel like taking off. Will she be able to be a happy, independent, free adult? Absolutely. In terms of hospitals, there's no reason for her to be in one. And according to Dr. Woo, Sparrow isn't suicidal and doesn't need medication at the moment. Which is a good thing since . . ." She looks at me, head tilted, eyebrows arched, like, *You're not getting out of this one.*

"I never took them."

Mom looks *pissed.* "What did you do with those pills I gave you every day?"

"I put them in my pocket and threw them out."

"Sparrow!"

"I know, Mom, I'm sorry. They were making me so dopey, and I was falling asleep in class and then not sleeping at night and I'd just be up for hours and it sucked."

She shakes her head, not like she's angry, but like she's been wandering around for an hour looking for glasses that were on her head the whole time. A piece of hair has become untucked from behind her ear.

"Okay," she says. "Is this flying still happening?"

"I can't anymore. I haven't been able to since I started talking about it."

"Why did you do it? Were things that bad?"

I look my mother right in the eyes. I want to hold her hand, but it's back in her lap, not resting in between us anymore.

"Yes."

All the blood rushes to my face, as Mom goes very, very quiet. She closes her eyes. There are tiny tears seeping out from under her lids. She's crying. I feel like the worst person on earth. This is not a woman who cries in front of other people. She's not even a woman who cries in front of me. I wait for her to open them again, hoping that the tears will be gone. I want to look at Dr. Katz, to ask her what to do. But I can't look at her, I just feel my heart threatening to break my rib cage, and wish that I hadn't said anything, wish that we'd never come here. Finally, she opens her eyes, and the tears stream right down her face, no consideration for her privacy, for the fact that never in a million years would she choose to be sitting here, crying on a couch in front of her daughter and a stranger. She looks at me.

"Mom." And the tears spill out of my eyes too, just a mirror for her pain. "You didn't do this to me. You're not the mean girls at school; you didn't make me into some weirdo who doesn't know how to make friends. You're the good stuff. You're not why I had to fly." She stares at me that way I stared at Dr. Katz the day I told her I could fly, like if I'm lying, she'll turn to ash. She runs a quick hand over her face and makes a grasp for Business Mom as she turns to Dr. Katz.

"And you're telling me this is normal?"

"I am telling you that escape or checking out is a common response to emotional trauma and anxiety, like the kind Sparrow experiences in social situations, like school."

"Is it dangerous? What if she had actually stepped off the ledge?"

"Sparrow?"

"I was just waiting for the birds to come and get me. I wasn't going to step off." I know the difference, I think to myself, remembering the time on the roof a few weeks ago.

"I'm sorry, Mom." And she breathes deeply. I say, "I've missed you so much." I can see her work at something close to a smile. She may have stopped crying, but I can't. My shirt is wet.

"Do you think you'll start turning back into a bird?" she asks.

"Honestly, I don't know. I still want to, if that's what you're asking. But in the meantime, I'm trying to figure out how to deal with things down here. That's why I'm screwing up so much at school. It's a lot harder since I can't fly away in the middle of the day. I used to be able to have energy to do work; I used to like it. But I also used to go to the roof at lunch every day and escape. I'm trying to learn how to do one without the other, but it's not going that well."

"Let's just get you through this year on the ground, okay?" says Mom. She sends a full Mom smile over to me.

"Hopefully," Dr. Katz says, "Sparrow can get some tools to deal with her feelings of isolation and anxiety, and she won't need to fly. That's what we're trying to work on here."

"That sounds like good work," says Mom. It's the closest

thing Dr. Katz is going to get to a thank-you, so she better take it.

"It's helping," I squeak out.

"I'm glad, baby."

I look at her now, my full face to her full face. Her arms are uncrossed. Her hand is near enough to mine to take it. She might be the person who taught me not to let people in, and the thought of letting her in seems impossible, but I take it. The pit in my stomach becomes just a little smaller. Just smaller enough so I don't think I'm about to fall in and keep falling.

20

I wake up with my heart beating fast, not like flying, kind of like a roller coaster. Like when you're stuck hanging upside down on a roller coaster and they're announcing technical difficulties. Tonight is the talent show, and this is, after all, a school for the arts. I can feel the pressure of the Park Slope Stage Moms Who Try Not to Be Stage Moms from inside my room. I brush my teeth and run through the list of props and the names of the performers, what's the order, who didn't show up to rehearsal yesterday. It's not like I care about the talent show; it's just that I keep thinking about the lights being wrong or the sound going out and everyone looking at me like, *Sparrow, what are you doing? Why are you ruining everything?* and then I feel like falling out of that stuck roller coaster.

"Sparrow, you're going to be late!" Mom calls up from the kitchen. This is the one thing that's really better since we went to therapy. She nags me again. It feels like heaven.

"I'm coming!" I run down the stairs and sit at the island. She's put out cereal and milk. "The talent show is tonight," I say, picking at my cereal.

"Mmhmm." She's getting our cups.

She looks up from her tea, planting her elbows on the island and leaning toward me. "You're scared," she says. "But scared is just scared; it's like happy or sad or angry. It's just scared. What time does the show start?"

"Six."

"I'll be there."

"Are you sure? I know it's early."

"I wouldn't miss it. Now stop imagining that worst-case scenario in your head over and over. It's going to be fine."

Mom knowing what I'm thinking feels so good I let go of a breath I didn't even know I was holding. "Okay."

"Have a great day."

"Thanks, you too."

"See you tonight. Now go!"

The glow from an actual, normal conversation with Mom keeps me from thinking that the talent show might kill me, until about second period. It's during a lull in Mr. Garfield's class (shocker) that the roller-coaster feeling comes back. The bell rings, and we shuffle out and into the rest of the day. In English, Ms. Smith puts a hand on my shoulder and Post-it note on my desk. *You'll be great. RELAX.* I put it in my pocket, and even though I still think I'm only minutes away from losing my breakfast, I smile. I wish the day would just hurry up so that I can face my doom.

In the bathroom during lunch, I can hardly stand to stay in my stall. I have Weaves blaring from my headphones but I feel trapped, too big for this small green square. I shuffle through my backpack, past my sandwich (no way am I going to risk eating right now) and past my books, to the blue Sharpie I've had waiting at the bottom of my bag ever since I finished memorizing what I need for today. I find the peach poem on the wall, and below it I add:

> *I have seen them riding seaward on the waves*
> *Combing the white hair of the waves blown*
> > *back.*
> *When the wind blows the water white and*
> > *black.*
> *We have lingered in the chambers of the sea*
> *By sea-girls wreathed with seaweed red and*
> > *brown*
> *Till human voices wake us, and we drown.*

I like how it looks; it takes up a big part of the wall now, and I've had to write over some *RiRi is hotttt* to do it, but you can tell that it's been done by two different people. Most people won't even notice it, but I imagine the ones who will. I imagine a seventh grader coming in here for the same reason I did, and seeing that she has some company. That she's not quite as alone as she thinks she is. Maybe she'll find "The Love Song of J. Alfred Prufrock" and write down the stanza that comes before the peach one. I imagine a stall full of "Prufrock." I mean, I'm sure it'll be painted over by the end of the year, but a girl can dream. And vandalize, for a good cause. I take out *Perks* and let myself get lost for the rest of lunch. No more roller coaster.

Until showtime, that is. Ms. Smith and I spend an hour before the show making sure that the Hula-Hoops, magic hats, guitars, harmonicas, flutes, and playing cards are where they should be, and we go over the set list one more time. She tells me there have been a few changes—Leticia and her dance crew of popular girls will be going on first, Jayce has dropped out, and Tanasia is going to be performing in his place. We're just going to have to wing the sound and lights. As the room fills with performers and siblings and parents and grandparents and aunts and uncles, I start to feel that awful feeling again.

Ms. Smith sends me to the light booth. "It's time," she says. I see Mom come in just as I'm running up the back stairs. I see her look around for a seat. All the parents are chatting with each other; there's a cacophony of *Oh, Colette, how are Jackie's piano lessons going?* and *What do you think about the season they just had? Jake is becoming quite the soccer star* and *Which tutor did you use for the ISEE? Oh, reeeeally?* Mom avoids eye contact and finds a place a few seats down from a family taking up most of a row. She gets out a magazine (I can tell from here it's *Wired*; it's always *Wired*) and starts reading. She looks uncomfortable. And then it occurs to me, oh my God, she's *awkward*! It's kind of great to see her like this . . . like me.

Ms. Smith's voice comes in over the walkie-talkie.

164

"Sparrow, dim the lights, I'm about to start." I slowly bring down the houselights with one hand while bringing up the stage lights with the other. Ms. Smith steps out onstage to welcome everyone. There's a small squeak as she approaches the microphone, which makes my heart beat so loud I can barely hear, but I adjust it quickly, and no one seems to notice, or to be running up the stairs to ask why I'm such an idiot. She thanks everyone for coming, thanks parents and kids and the administration and whatnot, and she even thanks me for running the lights and sound, and she asks people not to take photos and to silence their cell phones and . . . showtime!

First up is Leticia and her group and they do a dance to "Fancy" because of course they do. Leticia is a great dancer, but it feels weird to see her onstage in booty shorts, and wearing bright lipstick, her curls pulled into a tight ponytail. She looks worlds away from the girl who curled up on a mat with me or waited in line for hours for her favorite author. She looks grown. We're headed for different high schools next year and I wonder if I'll ever see her again. That doesn't make me as sad as I thought it would, and that makes me sad. The girls all strike sexy poses at the end of the song, and I bring the lights down to transition to the next act. I bring them back up and cue the sound, and I realize that it's happening, just like Ms. Smith said it would. It's okay.

As Francis and Eric are busy guessing which cards the audience members have drawn, I hear footsteps up the stairs and Leticia appears breathless behind me.

"Sparrow," she says.

"Hey," I say, eyes focused on the boys.

"Listen, I just want to say I'm sorry."

"Okay."

"I miss you."

I look at her. I can still see the girl under the makeup and the push-up bra. I've been waiting for this moment for a long time. It doesn't feel like I thought it would.

"I missed you too," I say.

"You have to understand, I just have to be different around Monique and them. They don't understand me like you do."

"So to be friends with them, you can't be friends with me."

"No! Not at all! We just have to be, you know, kind of secret about it."

I hear the audience start to clap. It's the end of the set and I need to pay attention so I can adjust to Tanasia's act on the fly.

"You know, Leticia, I don't know a lot about having friends, but I'm pretty sure that part of it is that you're friends with them all the time. I'd rather have no friends than someone who's embarrassed to be seen with me."

"I'm not embarrassed; they just don't know you like I do."

"You don't know me. I have to do this now," I say, turning my back to her.

I don't let myself turn around again until I hear her footsteps on the stairs. I bring the lights down and wait for the tears to come. They don't. The ground feels extra solid beneath my feet, and a slow smile comes across my face as I bring a spotlight up on Tanasia, who is walking toward the microphone with a guitar.

Leticia might be the only friend I've had since kindergarten, and all I've wanted since the day Mrs. Wexler died was for her to say exactly this, and now that she's said it, the world feels exactly the same and her offer of friendship feels like a long-lost favorite sweater that's too small once you find it. I'm so surprised I'm not upset that I almost forget about Tanasia. I focus on the girl onstage, small behind her guitar, which is hanging from her shoulders as she plugs it into a portable amp. She plays electric, which is interesting; she always seemed more acoustic to me.

"This sound okay, Sparrow?" she asks as she strums a chord. I adjust the level a little and give her the thumbs-up. She starts to play and my jaw drops. I would know those three opening chords anywhere. Then she opens her mouth: "With your feet on the air and your head on the ground . . ." I laugh at the shock of it. The Pixies. Tanasia. The notes. I never would have guessed, but of course—a black girl with glasses and a love for the Pixies—she could see me when I couldn't see her. I throw a blue light in there just to let her know I see her now.

21

So, how have things been back at the ranch with your mom?" Dr. K asks.

"Back at the ranch?"

"It's an expression; it means—"

"At home."

"You just wanted me to know that it's what old people say."

"Yes."

"Noted. So?"

"Back at the ranch in Park Slope, Brooklyn, things are okay."

She's smiling. So am I. Things are so much easier when it's just us and our dance. Everything seems a little more relaxed. Her Converse have some paint splatter on them. "It's better. We're talking. I mean, not a lot, I am not exactly chatty anyway, and it's not like before, but I don't think it could be. But it's not bad, and that's a lot better than what it was. This morning I made her tea. She likes tea before a big meeting, which she had today. So I made her some tea. We ate breakfast together. It's not a big deal or whatever, but it was nice."

"Kind of a big deal considering the last few months you've had together." My face is hot. I feel a small ball forming at the back of my throat. I'm irritated that I want to cry. Why now? Why do I always have to freaking cry?

"What's happening over there?"

"I hate the fact that everything makes me cry. I had breakfast with my mom; what's the big freaking deal? Why do I have to sit in therapy and talk about it, and why in the hell do I have to sit in therapy and cry about it?"

"Correct me if I'm wrong, but have you been having a tremendously happy last few months? Or years?"

"Obviously not," I say through the tears that have completely disobeyed me and are now making their hot trails down my face.

"And in that time, was one of the people you could most count on in the world, in fact, let me say, the only person you could count on in the world, your mother?"

"Yeah. So? I haven't talked to her. And I am now. I know that already; why is it making me cry?"

"Because it's a big deal, Sparrow." She sounds almost angry, but I think she's just trying to tell me she means what she's saying; she's also using her hands a lot, which she seems to do when she's trying to make a point. The waves of her tattoo move slightly with her gestures.

"Because I lost her and this morning I got to have breakfast with her."

"Yeah, you're surviving. That matters."

"Can I put some music on?"

"Sure. You've earned it."

I smile a little and head over to the iPod dock. The first notes haven't even squeaked out before Dr. K is smiling and tapping her foot. "Weaves," she says, and I smile because I know she only listened to them because of me. I feel my head lean back, happy and light at the end when Jasmyn starts screaming. The silence after the song feels less empty than it usually does.

"Listen, Sparrow, I know this may seem like a random question, but the school year's almost over. . . ."

"Yee-haw, as we say at the ranch."

"What are your plans for the summer?"

"I don't know." I remember the flyer crumpled now at the bottom of my backpack. "There's this place that Mrs. Wexler wanted me to go, I think. I don't think I could do it, though."

"What's it called?"

"Nix Rock Camp? Something like that."

"Gertrude Nix Rock Camp for Girls."

"Yeah," I say, surprised that she's heard of it, and also not surprised at all.

"Mrs. Wexler had good taste. It's a sleepaway camp: You'd learn how to play an instrument, you'd take music classes and join a band with the other girls there. At the end, you put on a show with the songs you've written together. "

I can't say anything. It sounds perfect. It sounds impossible. Far away. Four weeks. Other girls. Mrs. Wexler. A show.

I swing from good to bad to terrifying to awesome and back to terrifying again. I don't believe I've actually managed to say anything, though.

"What do you think?"

"I think it sounds . . ." My eyes. Again. Who is this girl who cries all the time? "Great."

"The deadline has passed, but I know a guy. They'll wait for your application. Talk to your mom, and have her call me if she has any questions."

22

I wander through the day wondering how I'm going to say it. During lunch, I trace my fingers along the words *When the wind blows the water white and black*. I've been through a lot of rough-blowing winds. I can probably do this. I eat my sandwich and close my eyes. Let the ocean rage.

When I get home, I put on Courtney Barnett and sing at the top of my lungs. I love being home by myself. I know that it's supposed to be weird or maybe a little scary, but I love filling this empty house with noise. Mom comes home as I'm blaring my way through "Dead Fox." She turns the music down, and I'm grateful for the little act of Mom-ness. She doesn't think I'll kill myself if she turns down my music. Normal.

"Hi, rock star," she says.

"Hi!"

"You're really into this stuff, huh?"

"Kind of, yeah."

She shakes her head just a little, but she's smiling. "Okay. How was your day?"

"It was all right. How was yours?"

"Long. You look like the cat that swallowed the canary. What's going on?" Mom likes old-people expressions almost as much as Dr. Katz.

"Well . . ." I bring the brochure out of my backpack, trying to smooth it out. "I think I want to go to camp."

Mom turns her head to the side and looks at me with a half grin. "You. Camp. You can't be serious."

"I am, a little."

"Where is this coming from, Sparrow? My Sparrow hates camp."

"I know. And I might hate this one, but I think I have to find out. It was in a book that Mrs. Wexler gave me. It's a camp to learn to play music and join a band and whatever."

"Huh." She sounds doubtful. "How long is it for?"

"One month."

"Here in the city?"

"No, it's upstate."

"Sparrow, I can't take you upstate every day. I have to work."

"No, I know. It's sleepaway."

I can feel something in Mom stiffen. I've never had a sleepover, much less gone to sleepaway camp for a month, and we both know what happened the one time I did try and that was just for one night.

"I don't know, Sparrow. You're barely back to yourself. You're barely passing eighth grade. What if you have an episode while you're there?"

"By episode, do you mean flying?"

"I guess."

"I'm not going to. Nothing would happen if I did, it's not dangerous, but also, I can't anymore. Not even if I want to. Not even *when* I want to. I can still talk to Dr. Katz if you want me to. Maybe on the phone or something? But I have to try this, Mom."

"I just, Sparrow, I just got you back. I don't want you to go."

"I know. But I think I have to. I think I can't just stay here with you all summer, even if I want to. Here's the information. I have to get the application in pretty soon."

She sits at the island, taking the brochure from my hand. "I'm proud of you, Sparrow. I know you're scared."

"I'm really scared."

"Speaking of which, are you friends with the girl who played that song at the talent show?"

"Tanasia? No, not really." I don't say, *Tanasia? I sit next to her every single day in English class and ignore her even though she's obviously trying to be my friend and even though she's probably the only person at school I have anything in common with. I don't say, Tanasia? I haven't said word one to her since the talent show. I don't say, Tanasia? Every single day I tell myself that I'm going to say hi, that I'm going to write her a note back, and every single day I sit there and avoid eye contact.*

"Well, maybe you should be."

"Yeah, maybe."

"Okay, let me take a look at all this."

"Okay."

I go upstairs and breathe a sigh of relief. I take out my math packet and try to finish it. I only have two weeks before grades close and there's no way Mom will let me go if I don't, well, graduate eighth grade.

"So, I talked to my mom about the program," I tell Dr. Katz, the sunshine pouring through the windows, covering everything in her office with a hopeful gold.

"How did that go?"

"Not great, but I think she's going to let me go."

"Do you want to go?"

I take a second to think about this. I am scared out of my mind. I mean, really, who am I kidding? I was in a freaking mental hospital four and a half months ago—do we all really think it's a good idea for me to go skipping off to summer camp? Also, there will be other people there, and we all know how awesome I am at that. But here's this woman who knows exactly how crazy I am, and she doesn't seem to think it's a terrible idea.

When I imagine camp, it goes one of two ways. The first, it's perfect; it's like a version of Mrs. Wexler's library but with music. I learn how to play bass. I am weirdly good at it. I don't even need to practice, but I do. I practice all the time in a small room with big windows and hot afternoon light just like this one. Bass is the perfect instrument for me; you can barely hear it if you don't know what you're listening for, but the song wouldn't be the same or even half as good without it. It's the pulse. You'd think that was the drums, but it's not. It's the bass. And bassists are tall and skinny, like me. Well, except for the tall part. But in the summer-camp-library dream, I'm tall too. It's perfect.

Then there's the nightmare scenario. It's the Y camp overnight, but I don't get to go home. It's the cafeteria, but worse, because I expected it to be better. And worse because it's in the middle of nowhere and we have to camp and I didn't even bring a tent or a sleeping bag. A counselor lends me a tent, but I don't know how to set it up, and everyone already seems to know each other and they're talking and laughing and going off for an activity while I'm still trying to put together my tent, it starts to rain, and I just crawl between the flaps on the ground and wait. And then I become the girl who couldn't put her tent together, and at reunions in ten years, no one will remember my name, but they'll remember coming back to the campsite and finding me in a little soaking wet pile on the ground. I play the tambourine. They make me lead singer. No one wants to be in my group. The counselors have to make the other kids be in a group with me because that's what counselors do, but everyone knows the difference between wanting to be in a group with someone and being forced to be in a group with someone. They all hate me because they're being forced to pretend to like me, and every day the teacher is like,

"Louder, Sparrow. I can't hear you singing," and I have to sit with my tent neighbors at lunch, which is eight hundred times worse than sitting alone.

"Sparrow?"

"Hi."

"Hi there. What's going on?"

I explain my two scenarios; I start to fidget when I get to the part about sitting with the other kids at lunch, mostly so I can hide the fact that my hands are trembling.

"I see," says Dr. Katz slowly, forcibly suppressing a smile. Is she seriously about to laugh at me right now?

"What's so funny?" I ask, angry.

"It's not that it's funny, Sparrow. You just have a very vivid imagination. So, let's start with this: There are no tents."

"There aren't?"

"No. It's at a college campus upstate. You're not wrong: There will be some nature, but you won't be sleeping in it. You'll be in a dorm."

"That means roommates; that's even worse!"

"There's no getting around it, kid, summer camp definitely means other people. But it's other stuff too—the chance to learn something new, to get good at something that you didn't even know you could do a week before, to be exposed to new music and its history."

When she talks about that stuff, the music part, my heart loosens. I don't have to fidget anymore. Subtly, my fingers press down imaginary chords on an imaginary bass.

"I like that part."

"Right. So, what you have to decide is whether it's worth it to you or not, think about it."

"I will."

"But not for too long. If you're going to apply, you have to do it before next week."

It's late, and I know I should be sleeping, but I can't. I'm reading *The Perks of Being a Wallflower*, and Charlie is in the hospital. It's different than when I was there, but it's nice to think that another kid, even a fictional one, has seen the inside of one of those places. I let myself think for a split second that maybe there'll be a girl version of Charlie at camp. Then I think of the muddy, rained-on tent. I wish I could sleep.

The next thing I know, it's morning. I come downstairs and there's a whole big breakfast waiting. Mom is not a pancake mom, but there are pancakes and bacon and eggs and warm syrup. *Warm syrup?* Who does that? Something is up.

"What's wrong?" I ask.

"Wrong? Nothing, girl, I made you breakfast. A little inspiration. A little sustenance. A little bravery."

"Oh. Thanks." I manage a smile.

"Eat."

I do. I tear into the pancakes with the warm syrup, making

sure to drip some on my eggs too. She puts a cup of tea down next to my plate.

"So, what do I need inspiration, sustenance, and bravery for?"

She raises her eyebrows at me like, *Think about it.* "The application, remember? We're doing this."

"Oh, that."

"Yeah, that. Get the teacher recommendation and fill out your part of the form. Bring it to me this afternoon at the office."

"I'm going to need another pancake."

When I get to her office after school, I hand Mom the recommendation (Ms. Smith's, of course) and my part of the application. She informs me of her plan. "Okay, Sparrow. You sit here with James until I'm done at six. You need to get math and science done *tonight*. Enough excuses. We're not going for As here; we're going for done. Got it? We'll stop for sushi on the way home, and then you're finishing social studies. Am I clear?"

"Yes," James and I say in unison.

"Good. Get to work."

James turns his speakers on quietly, but I can hear that he's playing the Strokes, and I nod in appreciation of his efforts. "It's go time, kiddo," he says. We tear through as much of it as we can, James helping me with whatever math he remembers from eighth grade, tossing me peanut butter cups when I get a right answer. I am awful at science, but half of the packet is just filling in the periodic table.

"Let's go," Mom says, with one hand on her hip, her briefcase in the other.

"Thanks, James," I call over my shoulder as I throw my stuff into my backpack.

"Good luck, kid; eighth grade's a killer."

Mom orders sushi as we're headed to the train; it'll be at the house five minutes after we get there. It's nice to have Mom be Mom — everything scheduled down to the minute. On the train she says, "Get out your social studies."

"Mom, it's a ten-minute train ride." She cocks her head to the side, that infamous eyebrow raised.

"People with 4.0 GPAs can argue. People who are barely managing to pass eighth grade and who are begging to go to summer camp and not summer school take their work out of their backpacks the second their mothers tell them to." Fair point. I work until we get to our stop. If Mom had her way, I'd probably write and walk at the same time.

"Go sit at the island," she says as we get into the house. "This is a working dinner." There is no point in arguing. After dinner, I may beg for some music but that's about as far as I'm willing to push it and I need some time to perfect my strategy.

She puts out the dishes and I can feel her peering over my

shoulder to make sure that I'm still going. "I promise, Mom, I'm working!"

"I want my child to pass the eighth grade; she acts like I'm a prison warden," she says to no one in particular. After dinner, she checks my work from the afternoon while I try to finish my *Gatsby* reading for the next day.

Around ten, I'm having trouble keeping my eyes open. "Mom, I'm tired. Can I put some music on to keep me up?"

She looks at me askance, trying to tell if I'm trying to get away with something or if I'm for real. "Okay, but go easy on me. No angsty white boys."

"You're the one who listens to NPR all day, home of angsty white boys."

"I like them for news."

"Here, try this." I put on Alabama Shakes. "A black lady indie rocker, and only a little angsty."

"Not bad," she says, tapping her manicured nails on the countertop. I get back to work. My head is too heavy to carry by twelve thirty. It's rolling around on my shoulders.

"I guess we could call it a night."

"I think I'll pass," I say.

She turns her chair toward me. She cups my face in her hands. "This is the last time, Sparrow. We're not doing this again. We're not doing hoping for Cs. We're not doing rooftops. We're not doing hospitals."

"I know," I say, lids half-closed.

"You want to go to camp? That's fine. But you need to be able to stay there, just like you need to be able to go to high school in the fall. And if Dr. Katz isn't helping you do that, we need to find you someone who will."

"She's helping, I promise," I say, wanting to talk about anything other than this.

"She better be. Sparrow, I'm serious. If you're going to camp, you're staying there. You've got to figure out how to beat this thing. I can't bail you out. Got it?" I pretend to be asleep, as my heart starts kicking quietly against my ribs.

PART 3

23

Mom and I pull up to the campus and there's a big banner that says WELCOME TO GERTRUDE NIX ROCK CAMP FOR GIRLS. Mom puts her hand on my shoulder as she turns the wheel like, *Here we go*. She parks the car and the entire time I think, Let's just turn around, let's just leave.

"Honey, you're going to be okay. Come on," Mom says. Possibly she can hear my thoughts, or more likely, I look like I'm about to puke. She takes my backpack out of the trunk and passes it to me. She'll roll the big suitcase. She must feel bad for me. Mom believes that you should only pack what you can carry. Right now, I must look like I could carry a water bottle.

We follow signs to this long line and my heart starts to beat a thousand miles a minute and I grip my backpack with both hands to keep from falling over. All the other girls seem to know each other already. They're running around and hugging and shrieking, and it's the first day of kindergarten all over again, except this time there's no Chocolate and no cubbies. Counselors are coming up and down the lines introducing themselves; the girls seem to know all of them too. A woman with curly green hair and another with a shaved head and a cheek piercing that hurts to look at are heading to me and Mom.

"Hi!" they say in creepy unison.

"I'm Ginger," says the green-haired one.

"I'm Jane," says the shaved head.

"It's nice to meet you," says Mom, who has apparently become an entirely different person and seems totally at ease in this super-weird situation. "I'm Donna and this is my daughter, Sparrow." Donna. My mother just introduced herself as Donna.

"Hey, Sparrow!" says Ginger. "Cool name." I think I manage to nod my head. I do not manage to look up. I am expecting a soft elbow in the ribs from Mom to get me to look them in the eye. Instead, she puts her hand on my shoulder. "She's a little shy," she says. Camp is apparently an alternate universe.

"I am too," says Jane. I don't buy it. Shy people don't shave their heads. "The shaved head's just a ruse," she adds. I smile a little bit, not that either of them can see it, since my eyes are glued to my shoelaces. They continue down the rest of the line.

"It's going to be okay," Mom says. I think she's said it about eight million times in the last twelve hours. I look up and up for the birds, just to see if I can do it. I close my eyes and wait for the *swoop swoop* feeling that I know won't come, and it doesn't. Mom says, "Sparrow, your turn," and puts her hand gently on my back to guide me toward the table at the front of the line. There are two more counselors at the front, registering people. The black one has almond-shaped brown eyes that peer up at me kindly from under a baseball cap. "Hi, Sparrow. I'm Ty. You're in Nina with me; let me show you where it is." I can't tell if Ty is a man or a woman, maybe something more like both. Ty is handsome and beautiful and takes my backpack with strong arms and leads us up to the dorm.

"Who's Nina?" I finally manage to ask.

"It's our hall. Every hall is named after an important female musician, like Nina Simone."

"I haven't heard of her."

"You will."

Ty takes us down a long hall with a brown-and-white linoleum floor. My door is the last one. There's a little bird cutout on the front that says *Sparrow* on it, and a yellow cutout in the shape of a spike that says *Spike* on it in black marker. Ty opens the door, and the room is tiny twin beds and nothing else except this girl and her entire freaking family and what seems like every instrument ever invented. She's setting up a drum set in the corner and has, like, four different guitars with their own particular stands and straps, and it's just me and my mom and my stupid pink rolly case that she got me when I was six.

"Hi," the girl says, bounding over to greet me, "I'm Spike."

"Hi," I say.

"This is Sparrow," Mom helps.

"Cool. Nice to meet you," she says. "Is it your first time at GNRC?"

187

"Um, yeah."

"I've been coming since I was eight. It's cool; you'll like it."

I don't know what to say, and so I say nothing. In my head I say, *Sparrow, how come you can't even carry on this simple conversation?* That doesn't help.

"Spike, give me a hand with the hi-hat, please." That's Spike's mom. Or . . . I think it is. There are a lot of people in this room. Mom is at my bed, taking sheets out of my suitcase. A girl comes by, wearing a ripped plaid vest and a white tank top, and jean cutoffs. I understand immediately that she's cool.

"Spike!" she shrieks. They run to each other, hug, do a chest bump, and then go into an intricate handshake. The other girl doesn't look in my direction. I usually like being invisible, but this doesn't feel awesome. "Come on, you've got to come say hi to Alyssa, she's been asking about you all morning." They scamper out of the room holding hands. Her family manages an awkward "Nice to meet you," and they leave too. They probably have their own friends to go visit.

Mom's made up my bed, and now she pulls me to it. She holds my hands in hers. She looks into my eyes. "You listen to me," she says softly. "You're going to be just fine, I promise. I know this is a lot of people and a lot of new things at once. I know you're scared. You're doing just fine."

My eyes start to water. "No, I'm not, Mom. I'm not doing fine. I can't even have a normal conversation with any of these people, and they all know each other already."

She wipes my tears and I feel like I'm about four years old. "This was always going to be the hard part. You just introduce yourself when people talk to you, and try to look at them when you can."

"God, what is wrong with me?"

"You're shy. You're anxious. Lord knows you come by it honestly. You've never done this before. I know you want to go stand by the wall like the first day of school but—"

"The cubbies. I didn't stand by the wall; I hid in the cubbies."

"All right, the cubbies. I know you want to go hide, but instead you're here. You've already won."

"It doesn't feel like it."

"Winning doesn't sometimes. Now, I should leave. So dry your eyes, and get ready to go to lunch. You can call me every day if you need to. I'll see you in four little weeks."

I nod. It's all I can do. I hug her with everything I've got.

She puts her hands on my shoulders firmly. "You can do this. You're already doing it." She kisses me on the cheek and closes the door after herself.

I lie on my bed facedown and cry for what feels like hours. After a while, I hear Ty in the hallway. "Food time, guys, let's go!"

I file out of the dorm with everyone else and head to the cafeteria, in a different building a few doors down from Nina. "Welcome to Heart, kids, this is where we eat. Go grab a seat."

Go. Grab. A. Seat. I hate those words. They make everything seem so simple when it's so freaking complicated. We all wait in line for food. It looks like there are hamburgers, veggie burgers, sweet potato fries, and cookies. I don't care, I don't have a lot of faith in my stomach's ability to hold anything down right now anyway. When it's my turn, I take some fries and turn around to face my doom. Tables filling up with girls who are chatting, smiling, finding a place because they know where to go. It's like everyone got a map but me.

Ty taps me on the shoulder. "There's a spot for you there, Sparrow," and points me to a table that's half-filled with girls. I walk over because what else can I do? I sit down. Conversation stops. I should never have come. "Hi," they say. They. It's like one big talking girl head.

"Hi," I say, staring at my fries.

"What's your name?" the big girl head asks. I hear my mother tell me to make eye contact. I look at them.

"Sparrow."

"Cool," they say, and then they turn into seven different girls and introduce themselves. Liz, Lizzie, Katie, Kim, Maia . . . I am paying so much attention to looking at them and trying to seem like a normal person that I miss who the rest of them are. I smile as much as I can, which probably makes me look like a robot, and say hi again after they all finish introducing themselves, and then I kick myself for being such a weirdo. I turn my attention to my fries. Finally, someone approaches a microphone that I hadn't noticed was on the stage. I hadn't even noticed there was a stage.

She stands there for a second. She's small, white, not much

taller than I am, and just as skinny. She's got freckles and a long red braid down her back. She's wearing a polo shirt and khaki shorts. Honestly, she kind of looks like a dweeb.

Then she opens her mouth.

"WHO'S READY TO ROCK?" she shouts at the top of her lungs. Everyone who's been here before screams their heads off. Everyone else looks away awkwardly.

"Dammit, no. Too often girls are told that they can't, that they shouldn't, that they should be quiet and be pretty. People like Gertrude Nix, you might know her as Ma Rainey, were pioneers for girls making noise, and each of you is here because there's something in you that's dying to get loud, even if it doesn't have any words. Your feet might want to get loud, or your fingers, or your voices. So I'm going to ask you again, WHO'S READY TO ROCK?"

Now everyone screams. Except me, of course. But I want to, maybe. There's a tiny squeeze in my throat—is that the me that's dying to get loud?

"I'm Kendra; I'm the head of music here. We're going to break you up by age group. Eight to ten, you'll be over on the right with Ginger. Ten to twelve, you're with Jane. Twelve to thirteen, you're with me. Fourteen to sixteen, you're with Ty." I feel a little relief that at least I'm with Ty. I head over to Ty's table.

"Okay, guys, I'm Ty. My pronouns are he/him/his. I'm in charge of your age group, which means if you're having trouble with your band or on your hall, I'm the person you come to. Okay? What we're doing today is breaking up into bands. Ren?"

A tall Asian woman with a shaved head and glasses with round bright blue frames gets up. She has navy designs down each of her arms. I notice that most of the adults here have tattoos. "Hi, guys, I'm Ren; my pronouns are she/her/hers. It's nice to see all of you. Listen up for your groups." She reads a list of groups with four kids in each. Somewhere in there, I hear her say, "Spike, Sparrow, Lara, and Tanasia." Tanasia. My heart drops to my sneakers as I look up and see her. She's wearing her hair in two braids down her back, a white T-shirt and ripped jeans. She smiles at me and waves a little. I look back at my sneakers. I never talked to her after the talent show, and there were two full weeks of us sitting next to each other in English, her looking at me and me looking anywhere else. And now, of course, we're in the same band. With Spike. If this could get any more awkward, I don't know how. But I'm sure it will. It always does with me.

"Hey, Sparrow," Tanasia says as we head over to the table to get our classroom assignment from Ren.

"Hi," I say.

"Funny that we're both here, huh?"

"What?" I'm so distracted and nervous I feel like all the blood in my body is rushing through my ears; I can barely hear her.

"Never mind."

"Y'all," says Ren, "these are your bandmates. You do not

have to like each other, but you do have to love each other and you have to support each other fiercely. Your day works like this. Every day, you will have practice together for two hours—an hour of songwriting and an hour of playing together. You will then have an hour and a half with the other people who are learning the same instrument as you. Depending on the day, you will have a workshop in the morning or the afternoon about leadership or women in rock history. You will eat breakfast with your hall for the next three days. Then, it's breakfast, lunch, and dinner with your bandmates every day starting Tuesday. Any questions?" There are no questions. "Okay, then, counselors, grab your bands. Let's do this thing." She looks down from her perch on the table to me, Spike, Tanasia, and Lara. "You guys are with me."

Ren takes us to yet another building. I'm starting to think that I'll never learn my way around this place. Then I would just have to stay in my room the whole time. "Guys, this is ESG; we're on the third floor." At least the building is named for music I like; maybe it's a good omen. I'll take what I can get right now. We head up to the third floor.

"Okay," says Ren, unlocking the door to our classroom. "You're a band; you're going to get to know each other real, real well. But first, we're going to brainstorm." On huge pieces of paper stuck to the walls we each write down what we think of when we think of rock and roll, who our favorite bands are, and what instruments we know how to play or would like to know how to play. This is easy; it's even a little fun. I like the ones on the rock-and-roll sheet—words like *heart* and *grit* and *power*. I add *hard to ignore* and *top of my lungs*. The bands are the same ones I would pick and I wonder if it was Tanasia who wrote down the Smiths. I add TV on the Radio and Patti Smith. On the instrument sheet, I write one word: *bass*. When we sit back down, Ren has us introduce ourselves by our names and our halls. Tanasia lives on Palmolive and Lara lives on Yoko. Spike, obviously, has the luck of living with me on Nina. Ren tells us that today is a short day because it's the first day (how is it possibly still the first day?) and so we're going to divide up by instruments soon. She asks who plays what, and Spike says she plays everything, and Lara says she plays the drums, and Tanasia obviously plays guitar. "And you, Sparrow?" she asks.

"I don't play anything."

"Ah, so you must be . . ." She's looking at the instrument wish list. ". . . bass?"

I nod.

"I can see that. You'll be a great bass player. Now, listen, guys, we have a performance at the end of the month. We have to take practice seriously, whether it's in band or with our instruments. This is what we're here to do. Tanasia, guitar is meeting on the second floor. Lara, drums meets right here with me. Spike, you'll go down the hall for vocals, and our brand-new bassist, you'll head upstairs to the fourth floor. I'll see you guys in Heart after practice. Dinner together, remember?" I groan, but I think I manage to keep it inside.

I go up to the fourth floor to meet the other bassists. Ty is standing outside the door. "Hey, everyone," he says, "let's do this." He unlocks the door to our room and turns on the light. There are six basses, one for each of us. The one I end up with is black and white with smooth curves and a red strap. I love it. It's mine. None of us is talking; we're all just trying on a bass, holding it, strumming it. None of has any idea what we're doing. None of us wants to stop.

"Okay, okay." Ty laughs. "I'm glad you guys are excited. Maybe we could go around and tell each other our names?" We go around. We've got Dina, Ana, Alexa, Lulu, Sienna, and me. We all live on different halls, except for me and Lulu. We exchange quick smiles.

"All right, obviously you guys are pretty excited to play. But first you have to learn about the equipment." Turns out I will not become a bassist today. Today I will learn about frets and strings and how to turn on an amp. Still, this hour and a half is the best hour and half I've had for a while. It feels like a totally different day than the rest of this awful day. Until, of course, Ty marches us all back to Heart for dinner.

Spike, Tanasia, Lara, and I all eye each other warily as we head to our table. Okay, maybe I'm the one eyeing everyone warily. Dinner is kale salad, chicken, and broccoli. Mom would be in heaven. I take some broccoli and wish I believed I could eat anything else without hurling. Lara has a loaded plate and two glasses of juice. She's chubby, but it seems like she hasn't eaten in weeks the way she wolfs her food down, like someone is going to take it away.

Spike tries to start up a conversation. "So, how was every-one's practice session?"

"Good."

"Good."

I just nod my head.

"Cool," says Spike, looking longingly at all her friends at the other tables. No doubt wishing that she were with them instead of us silent losers. Or maybe just one big silent loser.

"It's cool you're here, Sparrow," Tanasia says.

"You guys know each other?" asks Lara.

"We go to school together," she explains. I nod and look down at my broccoli.

"Cool," say Lara and Spike. The conversation stops. I cannot imagine doing this three times a day for the next four weeks.

After dinner, there is free time. Some girls take out their instruments and gather on the lawn to play together. Others cluster in groups, giggling. Spike doesn't even go back to our dorm; she's too busy with her hordes of friends, so I have the room to myself. It's seven thirty. Good enough, I think. I turn off the lights; I don't even change into pajamas. I just let myself fall asleep.

In the morning Ty wakes everyone up at six fifteen by blar-ing music. We all shuffle into the bathroom with our toiletry caddies. Some girls get into the shower right away; some line up by the sink waiting to brush their teeth. Friends make room for each other and share a sink. After the sleepiness wears off, everyone starts to chat. *Hey, can you pass me that? What did you do after dinner? Do you have the new Tune-Yards album? I need a new guitar, but my mom won't get me one. So lame.* Then there's the singing. The girls in the shower start a song and everyone joins in. It's too much like an alternateen *High School Musical* in here. I can't handle it.

I get out of the bathroom as soon as my teeth are passably clean. I don't even stop to pee. I go back to the room. No Spike. She's probably beatboxing for the shower girls. I dress and leave the hall as quietly as I can. Ty is nice and everything, but I don't want him to stop me with his kind eyes and ask what's wrong. I run down the back stairs and I push through the emergency exit door, hoping that there's no alarm. There isn't. The humid air hits me in the face. I thought fresh air would feel good, but now it's even harder to breathe. My feet carry me over to Heart.

At the back of Heart is a dumpster and some tall trees and some bushes that haven't been trimmed in years. They scratch my legs as I sneak past them. Heart has huge windows that go from the roof to the floor, but I duck behind the dumpster and into the bushes. You'd have to know to look for me to see me. Nobody knows to look. Between two scraggly bushes is a bench with cigarettes strewn on the ground. This must be where the counselors come to smoke so we won't see them. It's perfect. I lie down on the bench, breathing deep and looking up at the empty sky.

24

"Hi, Sparrow!" Dr. K says through the computer screen.

"Well, this is weird," I say. Skyping with my shrink from summer camp—I don't know a lot of other people who could say that. Then again, I don't know a lot of other people. Her hair covers the camera as she peers into the computer.

"You there?" she asks, in that slightly loud way that older people have when they use a new technology. Like she's trying to keep herself from shouting from Brooklyn to here. She leans back and comes into view.

"This is weird," I say again.

"I know. Just give it time. In a few weeks, you'll think it's weird that you won't have to turn on a computer screen to see me."

"Man . . . a few weeks . . ."

"Yup. So, what's it like?"

"It's only the third day, but I feel like I've been here forever. Even though each morning when I wake up, I'm surprised that this isn't a dream or that I didn't run away in the middle of the night."

"The thought's occurred to you, though?"

"Uh, yeah."

"What's going on?"

"Nothing."

"Okay, can you give me some basics? Your dorm? Your roommate?"

"I'm in Nina."

"Is that for Nina Simone?"

"Yeah, I guess."

"Have you listened to her?"

"No."

"Do it. Immediately. What's your roommate's name?"

"Spike."

"Really?" Dr. Katz laughs, maybe a little harder than she means to.

I smile. "I'm sure her parents didn't name her that. I'm sure her name is Mary or Becky or Staci or something, but she goes by Spike — even her mom called her that."

"So, how are you guys getting along?"

"She knows everyone here already. Apparently she's been coming here since she was in diapers. We haven't spent much time together. She stays in her friends' rooms until lights-out — staying away from the weird girl, I guess. By the time she comes back, I'm asleep."

"What about in the mornings?"

"Um." I can tell I'm about to get into some trouble. "Well, the first day I got up with everyone and there was this crazy line for the shower, so now I wake up really early, bring my clothes to the bathroom, change when I'm done with my shower, and then go back to the room." I decide this is close enough to the truth.

"Do you and Spike talk then?"

"No, she's still sleeping."

"Sparrow, how early are you getting up?"

Crap. "I don't know."

"Yes, you do."

"Yes, I do. I get up at four thirty. Regular wake-up is six thirty, so when I'm done with showering or whatever, I get back into bed and pretend to sleep until Spike gets up at six thirty with everyone else and leaves to brush her teeth in unison with her eight million best friends."

"Then what?" It is not a good sign that Dr. K knows there's more.

"I leave while she's out of the room."

"To go to breakfast?"

"Yeah."

"Yeah?"

Ugh. "No." I pause, sigh. "Breakfast starts at seven fifteen, so for that half hour I go sit behind the cafeteria, on a bench there behind some bushes. There are always new cigarette butts on the ground; I think it's where the counselors go to smoke so we can't see them."

"So, you go hide under the coats by the cubbies."

"Basically."

"Sparrow—"

"I know! I know, okay?"

"Okay. What do you know?"

"I know that is exactly what we talked about. I know I'm doing my stupid crazy thing in the same stupid crazy way. I'm hiding in the bushes; you think I don't know that's weird? That no one wants to be friends with the girl in the bushes?"

"It's not that no one *wants* to be friends with her, Sparrow."

"Then what is it?"

"Nobody can be. She's hiding in the bushes."

"Yeah, well, I don't care about the friend thing. It's not like I have much to compare it to. I was just hoping this wouldn't be the same. But instead of Monique, it's Spike, and instead of lunch anxiety, it's breakfast anxiety. It's all just the stupid same."

"Well, maybe. But the thing that sounds the same to me is you."

"I'm not turning into a bird."

"No, but you're trying to bolt. You're scared. Which means you're also angry, which means you're about halfway through stacking up those bricks, one on top of the other until you're the only person inside four tiny brick walls."

"I like the walls."

"Do you?"

"Well, I like them more than I like feeling this. The world isn't your office."

"No, but it's not a shark tank either."

"It feels that way."

"That it does. I want you to try something. I want you to look for someone who seems like maybe not a shark. Look for something familiar. Maybe she's wearing a Smiths T-shirt, or maybe she said something in class that you thought was cool but not enough people were listening, or maybe she seems shy and that feels easy; maybe she has Chocolate's kindness or my loud laugh. Whatever it is, sit next to her. Can you try that?"

I nod.

"Okay, that's our time, Sparrow. I'll see you on here next week."

25

The next day, I make myself sleep until six. I apologize to Dr. Katz in my head, but there's no way I'm brushing my teeth and taking a shower and doing harmony on a screeching rendition of a Blondie song. In my head, I promise her I won't leave the hall until breakfast. I open the door and walk to the bathroom.

"Hey, early bird." Ty is plugging his iPod into the dock to get ready to wake the hall up. I smile vaguely in his direction, trying to fake sleepiness.

"Just looking for my worm," I say, continuing into the bathroom and hoping I didn't sound like an idiot. I brush my teeth, take a shower, and start back to the room as Ty is kicking up the volume on the dock. The voice reaches me first. The first line stops me in my shower-shoe tracks. *Bird flyin' high, you know how I feel.* My hand goes to my lips, like the words just flew out of my mouth instead of hers. Then come the horns, and my head starts to go with the beat. I turn back to Ty.

"Who is this?"

"Miss Nina Simone."

203

"Oh." I feel stupid; I should have known that.

"Always Nina Simone."

MOVE YOUR FEET, I tell my brain, and I walk back to the room. *It's a new dawn, it's a new day.* Oh, Nina. I hope you're right.

"Good morning," says Spike, pulling herself up from her pillow. Her legs are sticking out of her sheets, and I can see the plaid boxer shorts she wears for pajamas. I turn away.

"Morning," I say back.

"Fancy seeing you here."

I don't say anything. I start picking out my clothes for the day, pretending to consider my options very, very carefully so that I don't have to go through the awkward dance of trying to get dressed with another person, a stranger, in the room. Spike hops out of bed, blond hair pointing in a million directions, throws a towel over her shoulders, and heads off to the bathroom in nothing but her boxers and a tank top. She doesn't even wear shower shoes. We could be more different, I guess, but it's hard to imagine how.

While she's out, I throw on my jeans and a T-shirt. I grab my hoodie. It's July, it's hot, but I can't really imagine leaving the room without it. I look at myself in the mirror, clutching my worn blue hoodie in my hand. I look like a little kid with a security blanket. Close enough, I guess. I sit on the bed until Spike comes back from the bathroom. She drops her towel and throws on another pair of boxers and a sports bra. I lie on the bed and try to give her privacy, even though she obviously doesn't want any. I could use some, though.

"Hey, first-timer," she says.

"Yeah?" I ask hesitantly.

"Time for the Hall Sing."

I sit up. She's wearing black jeans and a T-shirt with a denim vest. She's pointing to the door.

"Yeah, right," I say. Clearly, she's trying to trick the new girl, but when I catch a glimpse of her face, she's got a smile on and she's looking at me like, *Dude, I'm just trying to help you here.*

"Suit yourself." She heads out the door, leaving it open.

Soon I hear Ty's voice. "Good morning, Nina!"

"GOOD MORNING!" everyone shouts back. I get out of bed. I go to the doorway, and see everyone sitting outside their rooms on the floor, looking at Ty. I try to sit down without anyone noticing, but Ty sees me and shoots me a wink. "Welcome, everyone"—was there an emphasis on *every*one?— "let's get this day started. What do you say?"

"YEAH!!!!" There's a lot of screaming at tops of lungs for 7:00 a.m.

"All right, let's go. I want to hear y'all!"

Simple piano starts. The girls around me are snapping their fingers in time. They all know this song. I look around nervously, but then there's that voice again. The song is happy, but there's a sadness in her voice that settles right on top of me. *I've got you*, she seems to say. I close my eyes. My head bobs

205

back and forth. The girls around me are singing louder and louder; they don't care how good or bad they sound.

"EVERYONE!" Ty shouts over the music. *Every*one.

"And I'd sing 'cause I'd know how it feels to be free!" The music dies down and I open my eyes.

"Let's have a good day, guys. Eat 'em up!" Ty says, holding the hall door open for us to file out.

"YEAH!" They all shout, high-fiving Ty as they leave. When I get to the door, he grabs my hand for a second and whispers, "That wasn't so bad, now, was it?"

At breakfast, there's more music. A different band gets to DJ every morning. Today they're playing Bikini Kill. I let "Rebel Girl" distract me from my general hatred of cafeterias and my particular dread about sitting with the band. I get cereal and a cup of tea and head to my table.

"Hey, Sparrow!" says Lara, who's there early with a doughnut and a bagel. She seems kind of happy to see me. Her face is wide and open, her blue eyes blinking at me.

Spike sits down next, eggs and toast with a cup of coffee. Something about Spike always seems just a little more grown than everyone else, even her breakfast seems confident. It's annoying.

"Hey, roomie. Hey, Lara."

"Hi," we both say. I look down.

"Lara, how's drums?"

"It's good, we started yesterday with the kit. I have these awesome sticks from home that . . ." I'm not tuning out, just relieved that they're going to carry the conversation. While they're debating the relative merit of different drummers, Tanasia sits down.

"Hey," she says.

"Hi."

"How's breakfast?" I nod, looking at my soggy cereal. "Forget it, Sparrow," Tanasia says, a sharp tone in her voice that I've never heard before, catching me off guard.

"What?" I ask, looking up.

"How freaking hard do I have to try with you?" I have no idea what she's talking about. I thought we were just eating breakfast. "Months I've been trying to get you to talk to me, months. Maybe, I thought, she doesn't know the notes are from me, maybe she didn't hear me play the Pixies at the talent show, then we were here and I thought maybe you'd relax and give me a chance. But nothing. You pretend you don't even know me. You're too good for me? That's fine. Enjoy your breakfast."

Tanasia goes and sits at the other end of the table, on the other side of Spike, who has paused her conversation with Lara about the djembe to raise her eyebrows at me. I want to run to the bathroom, but I can see Ren eyeing us suspiciously. Kendra appears onstage.

"ARE YOU READY TO ROCK?!" she shouts. Everyone

shouts back at her, top of their lungs, arms in the air, every-one but me. No one is looking around awkwardly anymore like they did on the first day, no one but me. I am trying my hardest not to cry, not to run away. When we break for class, I casually walk to the bathroom. Why did I come here? Who do I think I am? I'm the kid who comes home from camp. Tanasia is the closest thing that I've had to a friend in almost a year, and just by being my awkward, difficult self I've ruined that too. How did I ever think that coming here would fix this? There's no fixing this. I take out my phone to text Mom. Then I hear her voice: *I'm not coming to get you. I'm not bailing you out this time.* I put my phone back in my pocket. Three more weeks seems like an eternity; Mom feels a thousand miles away. I sink to the floor. I hear Ty's voice through the door. "Sparrow, move it. Bass time."

I drag my feet getting to Instrumental, but I grow an inch just walking into the room. We all turn on our amps and set to tuning our basses like Ty showed us the first day. Sienna still has trouble hearing the low tones, so Ty helps her while the rest of us play around. Ty starts us out with some old Sonic Youth videos on YouTube. We can see Kim Gordon's hands really clearly. Ty explains that too often we don't just let our-selves play. We insist that we'll play once we know how, once we're perfect. He tells us that rock is about letting yourself learn by doing, not by waiting. He plays "Teenage Riot" through a few times, and we hum along with the bass line, try-ing to get it in our heads. After we can sing it, he tells us to play it. He runs the video again, and we sit holding our basses, disconnected from the amps, just trying to play along. When we start to get the hang of it, we plug in the amps. "See what happens," he says. "There's no wrong here."

The leather strap rests heavy on my shoulder, like a hand, like a guide. I can't tell my notes from Lulu's or Alexa's and it doesn't matter. I press down on the strings, not too hard, not too soft, "with purpose," like Ty told us. I strum the strings and tap my foot, and I don't even realize that I'm smiling until Ty is smiling back at me, saying, "That's it, Sparrow. You can tell you've got it, right? You can feel it!" I can. I've got it. I feel it. I don't want to stop. It makes me feel like breakfast was a lifetime ago.

The rest of the day goes by slowly after the rush of Instrumental. At lunch we have a presentation on Kathleen Hanna, so it doesn't matter that Tanasia will never speak to me again because there's no talking anyway. Tonight after dinner they're going to show *The Punk Singer,* so at least those hours will be filled and I won't have to sit in bed thinking about all the rooms that Spike walks so easily in and out of, filled with friends who want to see her, while I read and miss home and think about how I'm incapable of having friends and how angry Tanasia was this morning and wish for the relief that comes with a bass in my hand.

There's still the matter of dinner, though. At dinner I have a hot dog; Lara has two hot dogs and two bowls of ice cream. Tanasia waits until Spike sits, and then sits on the far side of

Lara. Spike concocts what looks like a gourmet meal out of the regular offerings of the cafeteria. She's toasted her hamburger bun and smeared avocado on each side, added red onions from the salad bar and what I think are sunflower seeds. She's made a salad with beets and cucumber, and a hard-boiled egg, and in a little paper cup I see that she's made her own dressing.

"You're like a gourmet cook," says Lara when she sits down.

"I dabble," says Spike. Three of her friends come up to the table, and they talk and laugh and punch each other on the shoulder and add each other to Spotify playlists. The other three of us look at our food in silence, until Ren takes the stage.

"ARE YOU READY TO ROCK?!" she shouts. Not really, I think. Everyone shouts back at her.

"All right, all right." She laughs. "Sing-along time, folks! In honor of Miss Kathleen Hanna let's start with this." She dims the lights and the screen comes down, and suddenly we're all screaming along. I can't help it. I'm singing along. I'm singing at the top of my lungs. So is everyone else. I'm just one more happy, shouting voice, we're like waves in the ocean, one on top of the other, impossible to tell apart.

26

"Hi, Sparrow." This time Dr. K seems to have grasped the concept of Skype. She's not yelling through the screen anymore.

"Hi." I feel out of practice. I feel like a hundred years have gone by since my last session. I don't have anything to say. I just wish I could carry her around in my pocket; that way I wouldn't have to talk. She would have seen and heard all of it already. She would already know.

"I was almost late to get here," I say, a pathetic attempt at a conversation starter.

"Oh? What held you up?"

"Class. I was playing and I lost track of time."

"Did they give you the bass?"

"Yeah."

"Who's in your band?"

"Lara's on drums; Tanasia plays guitar. I know her from school. Spike, of course, she's on vocals, and me."

"You know Tanasia from school?"

"Yeah."

"How well?"

"I don't know. Well enough. She sat at my table in English. We were going to be friends, but I don't think that's going to happen now," I say, frowning a little.

"What happened?"

"She got tired of waiting for me."

"She wanted to be your friend." I nod. "But you couldn't let her?"

"I was going to. I just wasn't ready. Now she's mad. I blew the only chance I had at a friend."

"Have you tried to explain?" I look at her, pursing my lips like, *How dumb are you?* "Just a question!" she laughs.

"No, I haven't."

"You might."

"Sure."

"And how is clicking with your other bandmates going?"

"I don't know."

"Do you like any of them?"

"They're fine."

"Do they live on your hall?"

"Spike, does obviously. Tanasia lives on Palmolive, and Lara lives on Yoko."

"Where are they from?"

"I don't know. I mean, except for Tanasia."

"Why did they come to camp?"

"I'm not sure."

"Okay, well, find out and tell me when we talk next week.

Think of it as homework, Sparrow. You've got to practice, just like for bass. Do you like the bass?"

"I love it."

"What do you love about it?"

"It makes me feel like I'm not invisible, but not in a bad way like when people sing 'Happy Birthday' to you in public and you want to drop through the floor. It's like this heartbeat; it's where the music is stitched together. I know the drums do that too, but the drums are so hard and loud. They're like the needle; the bass is more like the thread. Done well, you don't even know it's there. Miss it, and the whole thing falls apart."

"Have you been going to meals?"

"Yes."

"In the cafeteria?"

"Yes."

"Good work. What time are you getting up?"

"Well, it's better, I'm getting up at six. I'm sorry, I just can't get with the group teeth brushing and showering and singing and togetherness. But I'm not hiding in the bushes, so that should count for something."

"Indeed. Who are you eating with?"

"Week two, start of a new hell. We eat all our meals with the band now, like it or not. It's perfect. Tanasia isn't speaking to me, Lara is in love with her ice cream, and I can see Spike's eyes darting around like she's just longing to be with her friends and be finished having to sit with the loser roommate and these strangers. It's like six kinds of awkward at once."

"Maybe she wouldn't be looking around if the people she was sitting with were talking to her."

"It's okay. Lots of times, there are performances at lunch or sing-alongs at dinner. That takes the place of a lot of the talking."

"Do you sing along?"

"I'm not very good."

"I don't think good's the point."

"It's not. Every morning we sing as a hall before breakfast; I didn't tell you about it before because I didn't know because —"

"Because you were hiding in the bushes."

"Right."

"Funny what you miss that way. What's the song?"

"Every hall sings a song from their musician before breakfast. 'I Wish I Knew How It Would Feel to Be Free.'"

"That's a pretty perfect song."

I smile a little. "I mean, the lyrics, though. I wish I could be like a bird in the sky? This song is my anthem!"

"Billy Taylor and Dick Dallas, it's like they wrote it with you in mind."

"Literally. We all had to pick anthems, and this is mine. Ren told us to pick a song as our anthem, to carry it around in our heads, let it change how we walk, how we talk, how we feel. To pick it up when we feel lonely, to turn it up when we feel happy, to let it be our witness. I like the idea of Nina as my witness. I googled her. She had such a sad life; did you know she was crazy?"

"Crazy's just a word. Nina was a lot of things."

"Yeah. It makes me sad that she never got to be as free as this song."

"Go find out some things about your bandmates. Stop wishing you could do all those things that you can do and go do them. And talk to Tanasia. She might not be quite as done as you think she is. For Nina, if nothing else."

"I'll try."

"See you next week."

The next day at lunch, they show a music video. It's Janelle Monáe's "Q.U.E.E.N." I love her style. It almost makes me consider trading in my hoodie for a tuxedo. I love her voice. I love that bass line. The crowd literally goes wild after lunch; we're shouting, "ENCORE, ENCORE!" and they play it three more times before they can get us to head to practice.

It's never hard to get me to practice, but we're supposed to be working on songs for our individual bands, and since we can barely speak to each other, my band obviously hasn't been writing a lot of songs together. I pretend to fiddle with the tuning, but Ty figures out that I'm stalling.

"No songs yet?" he asks.

"None."

"Hmm. So, what are you going to do about that?"

"We'll work on it." Famous last stalling words.

"Okay." He sounds doubtful. He should be; I am.

"Can I work on another song today?"

"Yeah, okay," he says, trying to hide a flinch as Sienna gets too close to her amp.

I put my headphones on and start playing "Q.U.E.E.N." over and over until I can hear the bass and then more until I can hum it. I unplug and play through the song with my fingers on the frets. The afternoon goes by in a flash. All I want to do is master this song. I want to be a girl in a tux playing backup for Janelle. A Monette. A whatever as long as I can be in the same room as that music.

There's open studio time tonight after dinner for bands to practice together; ours has elected not to (duh), but I go over to ESG, where the practice rooms are, and I find an empty one. I stand in the corner with my back to the door and I play "Q.U.E.E.N." until my hands are tired and there are lines on my fingers where I've been pressing the same strings over and over. The beginnings of calluses. I play until all the lights in the other studios are off and then I keep playing.

"Sparrow."

I spin around, pulling my headphones off of my ears and dropping my hands from the bass at the same time.

"Hi," I say to Ty, who is looking at me with a lot of concern. "What's wrong?"

"What's wrong is that it's ten fifteen and you were supposed to be on the hall thirty minutes ago and no one knew where you were."

"I'm sorry; I lost track of time." It's true. I have no other excuse. There's a clock over the door, but I'm facing away from the door. There's a clock on my phone, but it's been in my pocket since I set my music on repeat. Ty sighs, long and deep but not angry. "I'm glad you're safe. You know, if you'd talk to a few more folks, they might have been able to tell me where you were."

Ah, yes. The talk-to-people-Sparrow lecture that I've been hearing since forever. I nod. I find that most adults take a nod for agreement when really all I'm saying is *Yes, I hear the words that are coming out of your mouth*. Still, it works for them.

"You can keep your nod, I know you're not going to do it. I'm just saying, you might try to let some of these girls get to know you. They're not so bad."

I don't say anything. I busy myself putting away the bass and unplugging the amp.

"Why did you come here, Sparrow?" Ty asks as we walk out the door.

"To practice."

"I don't mean here tonight, I mean, why did you come to GNRC?"

"I wanted to learn how to play bass."

"Ha! Well, you've certainly done that in record time. But I think you wanted something else too. If you let a few folks in

217

on what's going on in that big head of yours, you might get that something else. It's not as out of reach as you think. Bighead." He knocks my head gently and laughs.

We've walked most of the way between ESG and Nina. The moon lights the sidewalks, and the night air feels good on my face. I roll the sleeves of my hoodie down and look up at Ty.

"Yeah, maybe," I offer.

"I'll take a maybe. You were pretty in the zone back there. What were you working on?"

"'Q.U.E.E.N.'"

"Ah, Janelle Monáe, the reigning queen of blerdom."

"What-dom?"

"Blerd, you know, like you and me." I look at him blankly. "Black nerd, bighead."

I smile. "I didn't know there was a word for it."

"For you? There's way more than a word, but that's one of them, for sure." Blerd, I think to myself. Anything that puts me in a group with Ty and Janelle Monáe is okay with me. I wonder if Tanasia knows she's a blerd too.

"How do you like Nina?" Ty asks as we approach the dorm.

"The woman or the hall?"

"Well, both, but the singer." He pushes open the door to the hall.

I look him straight in the face. "I can't stop thinking about her."

"Hang on." He ducks into the counselor suite near the door and emerges with a record, an actual old-school vinyl record. "Here, it's her concert recordings. She was amazing live, so honest, so pained. She was glorious. Take it."

"I can't accept this; it's too much. Besides, I don't even have a record player."

"Huh, that's true, you don't, do you? I'm trying to think where you could possibly play it. If memory serves, Spike seems to have a record player in that room of yours. Maybe you can open your mouth and ask her if you can use it. Hell, maybe the two of you can even listen to it together." I twist my mouth into one corner, like I'm trying to decide whether I want to smile or scowl.

"Nice trick," I say.

"I thought so," he says.

"You think I love Nina that much, huh?"

"I think you love Nina way more. Go to bed."

I walk down the hall holding the record in my hurting hands. For the first time since I got here, I think this hasn't all been a big mistake.

27

In the morning, I do my routine, get up before the rest of the girls and brush my teeth and shower. I can barely make myself sit through the sing-along. The second I woke up, I knew I could figure out the bridge in "Q.U.E.E.N." I just needed to get back to the practice room. Apologizing to Dr. K in my head again, I skip breakfast and go to the band room in ESG, where I'll meet Tanasia, Spike, and Lara for our regularly scheduled Awkward Time with Ren, who'll try to get us to bond while we don't speak to each other (not to be confused with Awkward Breakfast, Awkward Lunch, or Awkward Dinner).

I head to the corner and plug in my bass. I straighten up and let the strap settle on my shoulder. I put my headphones on and start playing. The first time through the bridge, I totally flub it. I'm at least two frets too high. When I try it a second time, I'm closer, and by the third time, I've got it down. My heart is beating in time with the song. I'm smiling to myself as I start again from the beginning.

All of the sudden, I hear drums. I won't let myself turn

around. If I do, I'll mess up the bass line and ruin whatever is about to happen—because something is definitely about to happen. I don't know what it is, but the little hairs on my arms are standing on end and my stomach feels just a little queasy. I know that's Lara on the drums.

Then I hear a voice, beautiful and low. It's Spike, she's singing, *I can't believe all of the things they say about me.* She knows the whole song. She sounds just like Janelle. She sounds like she's been practicing too. When we get to the bridge, she loses the time and gets stuck but then I hear *I ask a question like this,* and Tanasia has taken the mic. She has more than taken it. She's spitting the rap right into it, not missing a beat, an inflection, a single word. It's perfect. We're perfect.

I'm scared to turn around, scared this has all been a dream, scared they'll look at me and laugh and that the magic that's been in this room, raising my hair and twisting my stomach, will disappear when I'm not looking at the wall anymore. I have a choice: I can keep looking at my wall, or I can turn around. I can act like we're in this room together playing this song we all love, or I can stay with the wall, not the one I put up in my head, but this actual wall right in front of me.

I turn around. I look at them one by one, and they look at each other and at me, and we are all smiling. Something's changed. Then I see that Spike is wearing a Smiths T-shirt. It kind of seems like a sign.

I take a deep breath and say, "Smiths. Nice."

And she says, "Yeah."

And then Lara says, "Uh, yeah, guys, they're great. Did anyone else notice what just happened? Sparrow, where did you learn to do that?"

We all laugh. Together. "Here," I say, "I learned to do it here."

"Spike, your voice is so good."

"It's all right. Sorry I flubbed —"

"Shut up!" interrupts Tanasia. "It was amazing." And we all look at each other in silence, because it was.

At that moment in walks Ren, confused. "I'm sorry," she says, "I must be in the wrong room. I'm looking for a group of girls who sit in awkward silence and don't talk to each other."

We laugh and I pipe up, surprising myself. "I think the spell might be broken."

"She speaks!" says Ren with a smile.

We settle into our chairs, and I sit next to Tanasia. Ren pretends to be looking for a whiteboard marker, but really she's just letting us talk. We each say where we're from. Lara is from Connecticut and Spike is from a tiny town upstate. She looks down when she says it, like she's embarrassed, or maybe like she's angry. I turn to Tanasia and take a deep breath.

"I'm sorry," I say. "I knew it was you, the notes in English. Well, I figured it out after the talent show. That was the best — it's my favorite Pixies song. I've wanted to say something for months." Now that I'm talking, it's like I can't stop. "I just didn't know how. I wasn't trying to ignore you. I'm just really bad at, well, kind of all of this. I was so excited you were here, but then I didn't know how to say, hey, you're the only person I've wanted to be friends with at our entire school and now you're here!"

Tanasia nods. "I knew you weren't ignoring me at school," she says. "You were ignoring everything. I just wanted to ignore it with you. But I could never get your attention. And then we got here, and it was like it didn't matter, you still didn't want to be my friend."

"I did. I just . . . Tanasia, honestly, I didn't really know how." I sigh and look down.

"You're doing okay now."

"Okay, folks," says Ren, "now that this is a band, we've got some work to do.

ᵔ

At lunch, sitting together doesn't feel quite as much like a curse. It helps that Tanasia sits where there's a spot now, rather than just trying to find whatever is farthest away from me. We form a square. As we settle in over nachos and beet salad, I ask Spike how long she's been coming here.

"Forever," she says. "My town's pretty rough, that's why my parents have been sending me here since I was eight, so I could get away for the summer."

"What's so bad about your town?" asks Lara, a tiny sandwich of three nachos stacked in her hand.

"They just don't like me there. My parents send me away

whenever they get a chance. They want me to know there are places that don't suck as much as Cowtown, USA."

Tanasia looks at Spike with her head to the side, asking the question we're all wondering without using any words. "It's because I'm gay, they don't like me. Not all of New York is like Manhattan, you know?"

"We're from Brooklyn," Tanasia and I say in unison.

"WHO'S READY TO ROCK?!" calls Kendra from up onstage, and we're all back to screaming our hearts out and listening to our guest artists for the day, who happen to be Ren and Ty in a band with a few other counselors. We cheer until it's time to go to class.

⌣

That night, I don't go to open studio to practice. I sit in the room, put on my headphones, and play through the rest of "Electric Lady." I get out a piece of paper and start scribbling. It reminds me of being in Dr. K's office, listening to music and writing down my thoughts. It feels like a hundred years ago that I couldn't meet her eyes, much less open my mouth. I sit on the little balcony outside our room, my feet up against the metal bars. I watch the night settle over campus and for the first time I think, Maybe I'm brave. Weaves comes on and I get the first few lines of a poem in my head and write them down. They stare back at me, not offering anything else up.

I'm feeling restless
Reckless
Like flying up at night and never coming down

I let the words mix with the night breeze, Weaves playing off my balcony into the darkness. I get lost in the light from the windows making bright shadows on the grass. Maybe I would have finished the poem if I hadn't heard Ty call room check. I didn't realize how long I'd been sitting there. My legs are wobbly when I stand up to run to the door. I don't want Ty to worry about me like he did last night; also, I don't want to piss him off. In my stumbly rush, my paper falls from the balcony to the dark ground below. I try to grab for it, but I'm too slow and it's too far down. After being off the hall last night, I know there's no way Ty will let me go down and get it. I pray for squirrels to eat it or for a heavy rain tonight. I get to my door right as Ty is headed from our neighbors to us. Spike rushes down the hall from the other end and slips in.

"Right under the wire, Spike," Ty warns.

"Sorry," she says, and she does look sorry.

"And you, fugitive, glad to see you here tonight." I smile.

"Okay, that's it," Ty says, raising his voice to address all of us. "Lights-out in five. Good night!"

We close the door. "Where were you running here from?" I ask Spike.

"Open studio. Thought I might see you there."

"Nah, I stayed in."

She points to my headphones, which are still on the balcony and still playing; she can hear the tinny blare of guitars from inside. "What were you listening to?"

"Weaves."

"I love Weaves!" She's smiling, maybe talking a little louder than she means to.

"Hey," I say, feeling a little of the magic still in both of us from the morning. "Do you like Nina Simone?"

"Are you kidding? I requested this hall. There's no one like Nina Simone."

"Um, Ty gave me this record of hers because I love her, but I don't have a record player. Would you want to—"

"Play it? Yes!" When Spike is enthusiastic, Spike is very enthusiastic. She's a lot like a puppy, lots of energy, lots of love, just lots of everything. She grabs the record from my bed. "I love vinyl; it's such a warmer sound, you know?"

"Uh-huh." I don't know. My mom loves technology, always embracing the next new thing. It's like she doesn't want to get old, to fall behind. She had the world's first iPod, and now she has wireless speakers synced to her iPhone.

Spike puts on the record, and the crackle and hiss of the needle in the grooves sounds like a fire. Warm. Exactly the right word. The track starts, and you can feel Nina's voice in the room like a third person. She tells us, "The name of this tune is 'Mississippi Goddam.' And I mean every word of it." I like her speaking voice; it's younger than I thought it would be, but then the song is pulsing, her pain right under every word like always,

226

and something else, something stronger. She reminds me of Patti Smith, of those moments when we risk everything because we have nothing to lose.

When the song finishes, I look at Spike and say the world's least descriptive word: "Wow."

"Yeah. Did you know it was banned in Southern states? She could have gone to jail for playing it. She was brave."

"She was crazy."

"She was both," Spike says, a little sadly. We're in the middle of "Four Women," when Ty knocks on the door.

"Ahem," he says. "Lights-out means lights-out. It's past eleven." His voice is all stern and counselory, but his face tells a different story, an extremely-pleased-with-himself story. A stay-up-as-long-as-you-want story.

"Sorry," we both say as Spike makes a big show of turning down the music.

"Good night, troublemakers."

We close the door and I say, "Do you like Patti Smith?"

"I don't know a lot, just what they play here at lunch sometimes."

"Have you heard 'Pissing in a River'?"

"I don't know, I think I'd remember that."

I plug my iPod into Spike's dock and play it. We sit in silence and listen. I fold up my legs and rest my head against my knees. It's my favorite way to listen. When I look up, Spike has tears in her eyes.

"Right?" I say.

"Totally," she says, wiping a tear away when she thinks I'm not looking.

We stay up until 2:00 a.m. listening to music. I play the Bots for her; she plays me Gossip, Sleater-Kinney, and THEE-Satisfaction and we both geek out about our love for Sonic Youth. Finally, Spike says, "I guess we should go to bed," and we turn out the lights and while we're lying in bed trying to keep our eyes open for just another minute, Spike says, "Sparrow?"

"Yeah?"

"I'm really glad you started talking to me."

"Me too. I'm sorry I didn't before. You just seemed like—"

"Like what?"

"Like you had all these other friends. Like I was just in the way."

"I thought you didn't like me because I'm gay. I get enough of that at school."

"Honestly, Spike, I'm so shy it didn't even occur to me. I know that sounds weird, but I was just busy thinking about how awkward I felt, I wasn't thinking about who you like to make out with."

"I thought that's why you didn't want to talk to me. You seemed so freaked out by me."

"Classic mistake," I said, smiling in the dark. "I'm freaked out by everyone."

"Well, I'm glad you're less scared now."

"Me too. I'm sorry. I know I'm kind of crazy."

"Whatever. I think you're brave."

28

The next day at breakfast, Tanasia and I are the first two there.

"Hi!" I say when she sits down.

"Hi," she says back with a half smile. "I still can't believe you're talking."

"Me neither. We'll see if it lasts. While I'm in the habit, though, I just wanted to . . . Thanks for giving me another chance. I know I've had a million already."

She nods. "You better be worth it." She smiles.

"I'll do my best to meet your standards."

"Please do."

We smile at each other, and it is crazy to me that this is the same person who was sitting in English with me all year.

"So, what are we going to do about a band name?" I ask.

"Yeah, I have no idea. I guess we'll figure it out today with Ren."

"I can't believe the show is in, like, a week and a half. I could vomit."

"Nice breakfast chat, Sparrow."

"Well, you wanted me talking; this is what it's like."

We're laughing when Lara comes and sits down without saying anything. She pokes at her oatmeal.

"What's wrong?" Tanasia asks. Lara doesn't answer.

"Lara, I just started speaking; you can't stop now," I say, trying to joke her into talking, even though that's never worked on me.

"I'm just off today," she says quietly. "It's, um, my birthday."

Spike slides in next to her. "Did I just hear you say birthday? HAPPY BIRTHDAY!"

Lara turns so red you can't see her freckles. She looks down. "Thanks."

"Why is your birthday a bad thing?" asks Tanasia.

"I don't know. I've just never had a great one. I'm always away at camp for it. It's never that fun."

"Well, we could make this one fun." You can see the wheels turning in Spike's head as she speaks.

"So, you've been to GNRC before?" I ask.

"No, not this camp."

"Which one?"

"You wouldn't know it."

"Why not?" asks Tanasia. "I've been to three different camps before this one."

"I'm pretty sure you haven't been to fat camp," says Lara, pushing her oatmeal away. It's cold now, and a gross film has started to form at the top.

"Your parents send you to fat camp?" asks Spike, stunned.

"No, I'm sorry, not fat camp—True You/New You Camp for Health. Whatever. It's fat camp. Every year since I was nine."

"But you're not even that . . ." Tanasia doesn't know how to finish the sentence.

"Fat. Yes, I am, but I don't care. They do. Every year they send me and every year I have, like, a piece of celery with a candle in it for my birthday. It's the worst."

"Are they like that when you're home too?" I ask.

"Yeah. They're on me at every meal. I've got a meal plan I have to follow. They go through the trash in my room looking for candy wrappers. Being here is the first time I've ever been able to choose my own freaking meals. You might have noticed I have frozen yogurt at, like, every meal. The sweet taste of revenge."

"They don't even let you have frozen yogurt?" asks Spike, reeling from the injustice of it all.

"Spike, they don't let me have cheese."

"Damn."

"Wow."

"Okay," I say, "so it's your birthday. You're not at stupid fat camp, and you're not at home. You're not going to have celery. How do you want to celebrate?"

"Yeah," says Spike. "What do you want to have for your birthday? We'll get you whatever it is."

Lara laughs nervously. "I don't know."

"Sure you do," says Spike. "Think of something you could never get at home. What do you want, an ice cream cake?"

231

Lara is thinking. She squinches up her face for a second, and then it's like a lightbulb goes off over her head. "I've always been really curious about pizza."

"NO PIZZA? Where do you live, prison?"

"Kinda."

"You've really never had a pizza?" asks Tanasia.

"I've had those diet frozen pizzas, but they taste like cardboard, and they don't look anything like the ones they sell in pizza places. The melting cheese, the pepperoni." She's practically drooling.

"We will get you the best pizza in all the land!" says Spike.

During our afternoon session in band practice, Ren seems stressed. "Okay, y'all, it's time. We've waited as long as we can. You need a name. I mean, look, you also need a song, but let's see if we can't find a name for ourselves today."

"Well, I was thinking," says Spike, "we all love Janelle Monáe, what about the Monáes?"

"We can wear tuxedos!" adds Tanasia. Lara and I nod in agreement.

"I like it," says Ren, but she sounds doubtful. "The thing is you guys are your own band. You're not just a copy of an awesome band. You're your own awesome band."

"Maybe," I say, "but awesome bands have songs."

"We'll get there," Ren says. We all stare at each other

blankly. "Ideas?" she coaxes. More blank stares. "Okay, team, everyone take a square." She hands us all pieces of scrap paper. "Each and every one of you is going to write down three names. I don't care how silly they are, I don't care if you would never listen to a band with this name. We just need something to get us going. A bad idea can lead to a great one. Write down your favorite word or your favorite sound. Whatever. Just write. Three ideas. Each. Go."

After a few minutes, Ren collects our papers and writes the options on the whiteboard. "Okay," she says, reading through them, "we've got Phalanges, Sinners, Heartbeat, Ampersand, Tuxedo Girls, Hokey-Pokey — you guys are doing great on the words that are fun to say — the Lollygaggers, Eponymous (very clever), Phlebotomy, the SHEnanigans, the Fuddy Duddies and . . . wait, I can't read this word."

"It's mine," I say, looking down. "It's silly."

Ren rolls her eyes in the kindest possible way. "Come on, now," she says.

"It says Chachalacas."

"What's a Chachalaca?" asks Tanasia.

"It's a bird. It's this little bird with a skinny neck and a big body. They're not found in the U.S. except for southernmost Texas; they're mostly consumed for food and they reside in Central America and — "

"Wow, you're like a bird almanac!" says Lara.

There's an awkward silence where I know I've said way too much, revealed myself for the loser I am. I've barely been speaking for two days, and I've already ruined the whole thing. I'm about ready to curse myself out for ever being stupid enough to open my mouth, when Spike breaks the silence.

"I love it! It's like Boom Shakalaka! But instead it's Chachalaca!"

"We could be the Boom Chachalacas," says Tanasia. Her voice is eager, even enthusiastic. I look up and they're smiling and writing it on the board.

"I like it too," says Ren. "It suits you guys. A vote?" Everyone's hands go into the air before she even gets a chance to ask for all in favor. "It's unanimous, then—congratulations, Boom Chachalacas. You can start making your band posters this afternoon."

"I think we should still try to get some tuxedos," says Tanasia. "I mean, we won't call ourselves the Monáes, but we can at least pay our respects, right?"

"I think I can get us tuxedos," says Spike.

"It's better than dressing up like a chachalaca," I say quietly. "They're pretty ugly."

~

That night at dinner, we're all told to sit down and wait. Kendra lets us know that they have something important to discuss with us when we're seated. I look at my bandmates, confused. "Did we do something wrong?"

"Yeah," says Lara, "are we in trouble?" Spike shrugs like

she doesn't know but she sends a wink my way when Lara isn't looking. A minute later, barely hiding the glee in her voice, Spike asks, "What's that smell?"

"It's pizza!" cries Tanasia. "Like a lot of pizza!"

Counselors are going from table to table dropping off a box of pizza for each band. When they get to ours, the box is extra large, and when we open it, there's pepperoni on top that spells out *Happy Birthday!* We all begin to sing. Ren takes a candle from behind her ear and puts it in the middle of the pizza. Ty lights it, and when the song is over, Lara closes her eyes, takes a deep breath, and blows it out. When she opens her eyes again, they're a little watery. Her smile is so big it looks like it might hurt in the morning. She takes a hot cheesy slice in her hands and happily burns the roof of her mouth a little. "Thank you," she whispers to Spike between bites.

Lara comes into band practice grinning. "I think I've solved our song problem," she says.

"Here's hoping," says Ren. "What do you have?"

"Well, you know how Yoko is on the first floor? I woke up and found this sheet of paper pressed against my window a few days ago. Someone must have dropped it, but it has this awesome poem on it. I thought we could use the lines and start our song that way."

My stomach drops straight to the bottom of the world.

"Go for it," Tanasia says.

I look down, like I'm listening oh-so-carefully.

"I'm feeling restless, reckless, like flying up at night and never coming down."

I tell myself not to look guilty or embarrassed so that no one asks me what's wrong.

"Sweet. Let's each start writing from there and see what we come up with. Then we can combine, share, whatever," Tanasia says.

"Do you all feel like it's something you can work with?" asks Ren.

"Definitely," says Spike.

"Let's do it," says Tanasia.

I force my head to nod up and down and hope that will be enough for Ren.

"Okay, so what we need to do is ask at lunch for the next few days for the permission of the person who wrote it. We need to give them credit for their work."

We all start writing. Well, they all start writing. I doodle and try hard to keep my face from showing my feelings. The rest of the morning goes great — everyone writes their ideas on the whiteboard, and we join verses and borrow words from each other. By tomorrow, we'll have the chorus down and the bridge worked out. It's kind of easy, working together to get the best song possible, except for the pounding in my chest that will bang and bang against my ribs right through the rest of class and straight through lunch. When we make our

236

announcement asking the mysterious author of this wonderful poem to please come forward, I wish for back when a pack of birds and fifteen minutes of recess would fix everything. It beats right through that, and stomps through the rest of the day until bass class. I pick up the instrument like it's a life preserver. Because I guess it is.

29

I run in out of breath. "Sorry I'm late, I'm here."

"I'm glad you made it. Where were you?"

"You won't believe me."

"Try me."

"I was 'hanging out,' I think they call it, with Tanasia, Lara, and Spike."

"No, you weren't," Dr. K says with a grin.

"I was!"

"My goodness. What a week it's been. What happened?"

"I don't know where to begin. We started talking?"

"Wow, Sparrow. So, I'm guessing you know where they're from?"

"Well, Tanasia is from Brooklyn, obviously. We're going to the same high school next year. Spike is from upstate. She's gay, and it's awful for her there, so her parents send her here every year. Lara is from Connecticut. Her parents send her to fat camp every summer, but this year her music teacher convinced them to let her come here. She eats frozen yogurt at every meal. We all love Janelle Monáe. Spike and I love Nina Simone, and I played her Patti Smith."

"Huh. Sounds like a band to me. How's it feel?"

"Good?"

"Is that a question?"

"Yeah, I mean, I'm still not used to it. It's not like I'm talking to anyone other than these three people, but . . ."

"It's a start, don't you think?"

"I think it might be. It's hard to trust it. But I think I might be having fun. That's new."

"The girl I met in February didn't know how to have fun."

"It's cool when it's not scary."

"A start."

"Yeah. It's crazy that next week is our last week. Next time I talk to you it'll be in person."

"How does that feel?"

"You are such a therapist."

"Humor me."

"It's kind of hard to imagine past the show Sunday."

"That's the finale, right? You guys have a show?"

"Yeah, all the parents, all the kids, all the teachers, everyone. They even sell tickets to the community, like people who are up from the city come, the college kids in town, everyone."

"Is your mom coming?"

"Yeah, Mom, Aunt Joan, and my cousin, Curtis."

"Wow."

"Ugh."

"Fair enough. What are you going to play?"

"Well, we were having trouble getting started on a song, and then three days ago Lara comes in and she's like, I found the most amazing poem. She woke up with it pressed against her window. She loves this poem, but it's just the first three lines, and she wants to use it to start our song. So we get up every day at lunch and make this big announcement, like, 'Who wrote this poem? We love it and we want to use it in our song,' but no one has come forward."

"Because it's yours?"

"How did you know?"

"Part of the job."

"Yeah, it's mine. I was writing on my balcony and it fell to the ground right before curfew. I checked in the morning, but it was gone."

"And you didn't tell them?"

"Look, I asked some people where they were from and listened to a few songs with my roommate; I didn't become a different person. Of course I didn't tell them!"

"Are you going to?"

"Absolutely not."

"But you guys wrote a whole song based on your poem?"

"Based on three lines, yeah."

"I'm sure they'd like to know."

"Maybe, but I have to get through Sunday first."

"Will you tell me the lines?"

"Fine. It's just the few lines. It's *I'm feeling restless, reckless, like flying up at night and never coming down.*"

"Sounds like a pretty good start."

"Not really, I couldn't get the poem to go anywhere. I was going to throw it out, but now it's the first verse of our song."

"Well, I think it's a pretty great accident. I hope you tell them someday."

"We'll see. I don't need any bird questions, you know?"

"If they picked the poem, it sounds like they already know."

"You think they know?" I hear the tremble in my voice. My face is hot.

"I don't mean literally, but, Sparrow, if they picked the poem, it's because something in it spoke to them. You're not the only person who's felt restless or reckless or like flying away and never coming down. You might be the only one in the band who's experienced it, but they're trying to tell you they know what that feels like and they feel that way too."

"How do you know?"

"It's human. I don't think there's a person on the planet who hasn't felt that way. It might not lead them up to a rooftop, but when people hear your song, watch for the nodding heads. It's not because of the beat, or at least not only because of the beat, it's because they know exactly what you mean. You know that feeling, I know you do, when someone else says how you thought only you felt? You're giving that to people, you've already given it to the band, and on Sunday you'll give it to a few more."

"A few."

"Deep breath. You'll be great."

"Okay."

"Next time I talk to you, it'll already be over."

"Okay, right. Good."

"Sparrow, one more thing: Even if you can only do it for a minute, try not to fly away during the show. Stay there. You owe it to yourself, and you owe it to them."

"I can't fly anymore."

"You know what I mean. No checking out, no hiding in the bushes. Be there. You won't want to miss it."

"If you say so."

"I do. I'll see you next week."

30

The days leading up to the show fly by. We're practicing and practicing. Tanasia brings in a new song idea for the encore because Ren says that all bands should be prepared for an encore, even though we won't have time for one. We spend our mornings in Instrumental perfecting our songs and our afternoons in workshop, making Boom Chachalaca posters and T-shirts and figuring out how to get four tuxedoes by Saturday.

"I might have been a little overly optimistic," admits Spike the day before the show.

"Ya think?" Tanasia says, with a little edge to her voice.

"I just wanted to do right by Janelle . . . okay, and to wear a tux."

We're sitting among piles of T-shirts and markers and fabric pens, knowing other bands are already putting the final touches on their outfits.

"Well, we could make our own," says Lara, holding up a black T-shirt and a white one.

"I don't think making four tuxedoes by tomorrow is exactly a plan," Tanasia says.

"But what if we did it like this?" Lara says, grabbing some scissors. She cuts the middle out of a black T-shirt, making a kind of jacket. She draws a bow tie on a white T-shirt and then puts it on, slipping her arms through the black fabric. "I mean, I'm no artist, but it could work, right?"

"Don't give it to your boyfriend to wear to the prom, but yeah, I think it could work," says Tanasia with a smile. She slips it on over her tank top. We look at each other and nod, grabbing shirts and scissors. We work straight until dinner, our hands tired from cutting and making the posters and all the practicing we've been doing.

You can tell the minute you get to Heart that it's not just us—everyone is exhausted. Every single person in here looks like they could use a nap. Kendra seems to have other plans.

"ARE YOU READY TO ROCK?!" she shouts from the stage. Mouths full of macaroni and cheese, barely lifting our forks from the tables, we all manage a weak "Yeah . . ."

"Oh, this will not do!" she shouts into the microphone. "Can we do something about these sad sacks, DJ? We used to have a camp full of rock stars here, as I recall. I think we know what they need." Ty is in the DJ booth grinning. The bass line comes in right away; it makes my shoulders go up and down even though I thought I was too tired to move. I try to keep them still. "What do you want to do, Ty?" shouts Kendra over the music.

"I want to shoop!" he shouts. The chorus comes in and all

the counselors flood the stage shooping at the top of their lungs. They're showing off their dance moves, busted robots and the cabbage patch, and looking ridiculous. Then they spread through the cafeteria, grabbing us by the hand one by one and spinning us around. Ty comes up to me.

"You know I don't dance," I say.

"Mmmhmm," he says, taking my hand and turning me under his arm. "Oh, look . . . that's called dancing!"

I laugh at him and roll my eyes, and then the song changes. Everyone starts hooting and hollering as "Run the World" comes on—apparently everyone, even Spike, even Spike's coolest friends, loves Beyoncé. Lara is fist-pumping the air and screaming "Girls!" Spike is marching in place like a soldier in Queen Bey's army. I turn to look for Tanasia. She's in the corner, like she thinks no one will see her there. Her eyes are closed and her back is to us, the same way I play the bass. She's moving her shoulders up and down crazy fast, her legs are kicking up and down, taking her down to the floor and back up with the beat. She could be a dancer onstage with Beyoncé.

I approach her when she takes a break. "That was amazing," I say.

She looks away. "Don't tell anyone at school, okay?"

"What, that you're a dance machine who can do crazy things with her body and loves Beyoncé?"

"Yeah. Don't tell them that. I don't want to be like . . . you know . . . those other girls."

"Look around. Everyone loves Beyoncé."

"I know, but first those girls at school know that you have something that they want, then they bring you into their group just so you can teach them dance steps or whatever."

"Sounds like you're speaking from experience."

"Maybe."

"Leticia?" It's been so long since I thought of Leticia that it surprises me to hear myself say her name.

"Worse. Monique."

"You were friends with Monique?"

"For about thirty seconds in seventh grade, until she got tired of me. She realized that just because I'm a good dancer it doesn't mean I hate school or only like Juicy Couture or want to be mean to people. So, anyway, don't tell anyone, okay?"

"I won't. I will keep up your disguise as a big dork, when in fact you'd be like the most popular girl in school."

"I prefer dorkdom."

Lara and Spike come over just in time for "Independent Women" and we all throw our hands up at each other and laugh. It is maybe, *maybe* true that I'm dancing.

· · ·

That night, Ty checks us in and then tells us to go outside. We all look confused. "It's a ritual," he says. "The night before the big show, we go have primal scream to get all the nerves out." I look at Spike, and she says, "Don't worry, it's fun."

In the middle of campus, halfway between Heart and ESG, there's a flagpole with a big circular driveway around it. The whole camp is there, forming a circle in the driveway. As more and more girls join, everyone begins to hold hands. Lara and Tanasia find us; Tanasia takes my hand, Lara takes Spike's, and a minute or so later, the whole camp is joined together.

"Okay," says Kendra, standing in the middle by the flagpole. "You've all worked very hard. You've spent this last month trying to find your voices, learning instruments that you'd never seen just four weeks ago. You've taken strangers and made them your bandmates, made them your sisters." Squeezes from Tanasia and Lara on each side of me. "You have been fearless and brave and silly and curious. You have said maybe when everything in you wanted to say no. I've watched each and every one of you embrace your fierce, loving, rocking self, and I couldn't be more proud. And I know you couldn't be more nervous. But tomorrow is just another day. You've done all the work already. The hardest part is over. Whatever happens tomorrow, you are rock stars, you are heroes, and I am so lucky to know you. And you are so lucky to know each other." I squeeze back. "Tonight, I want you to let go of all of it. Let go of the nerves and the what-will-they-think, let go of any voices of perfectionism or criticism. We're going to open our mouths and scream because not everyone can make that kind of noise, but we can. And so we must. One . . . two . . . three . . ."

We hold hands tighter and straighten our arms all the way down. Like we could take off. Like one big mouth, we breathe in, open up, and let it all out. It feels like everything muddy, difficult, and dark inside me is coming up and out. I feel a flutter through my chest as it rises, and a force as it flies out of my mouth. Lara is screaming and smiling at the same time. I think I see a tear in the corners of Spike's eyes. They're closed and her face is red and it's like the scream is coming up from the very bottom of her insides. We all stop, as if by magic, at the same time. All our demons let loose into the night air, carried up to the stars that we can see so clearly here.

"I love you guys. Eat 'em up tomorrow. Now get some sleep." With that, Kendra dismisses us back to our dorms. Spike and I hug Lara and Tanasia, and we all say, "See you tomorrow," and even though my voice trembles a little bit at the word *tomorrow*, we put our hands in for a group high five.

Back on the hall, after Ty checks us in again, Spike and I both sit on her messy, unmade bed.

"You love primal scream, huh?" I ask.

"Yeah. It's always my favorite part."

"Can I ask you something?"

"Shoot."

"Were you crying?"

"Maybe. The end of camp is rough."

"Why?"

Spike sighs and looks at her dirty sneakers, which she's still wearing, which I try not to think about because — gross.

"It's hard. Going back is hard. Eleven months until I get to be here again. Until I get to have friends again."

"You don't have friends at home?"

"Don't sound so surprised."

"But you have so many friends here!"

"I've known people here for a long time. You guys are my closest friends, though."

"I don't have any friends at home either, but that's not much of a surprise."

"You do now. You have Tanasia. You're lucky."

"That's true. She'll be the first."

"I don't have a Tanasia. I have stupid boys who spit on me when I'm walking down the stairs. I have girls who leave the locker room when I walk in it. And if I'm really lucky, I'll have Derek again this year." Her voice is dripping with sarcasm.

"Who's Derek?"

"He's the kid in my class, in three of my classes actually, who sat behind me and whispered the word 'dyke' at me every single day for forty-five minutes all of last year."

"Did you complain?"

"I did. They told me that if it were true, a teacher would intervene. It just sucks." Spike looks defeated. She looks so small to me, this girl with the big voice and the big personality.

"I wish I could go with you," I tell her.

She smiles, resigned. "I wish you could too."

"You can come visit—come to school with me and Tanasia for a day. We'll take you around Brooklyn."

She nods. "I'd like that."

"Can I ask you another question?"

"Yeah."

"Why Spike? I mean, is that what your parents named you?"

"No, they named me something that wasn't going to help."

"How do you mean help?'

"Think about it this way: You're me, right? You're this gay kid in this tiny town, people want to mess with you. The whole point is that you need to be tough to keep people from messing with you. You need a name that will at least try to keep them away. Rosie wasn't doing it for me."

"Your name is ROSIE?"

"It is. Or it was, until I went with Spike."

I nod. "The thorns instead of the flower."

"Exactly. We've all got our ways of keeping people out, right? Want to play something?" She hands me a guitar and teaches me a few chords. She sings and I play until we fall asleep, shoes on, lights on, sitting upright on her bed.

31

The sound of Nina singing "Here Comes the Sun" wakes us up in the morning. We blink our eyes, and I look down at the guitar on my lap. The lights are on.

"Guess we fell asleep," I say.

"Yeah." She sounds like a talking frog.

"Whoa, Spike, your voice is so hoarse. Let's get you some water." We get up and go into the bathroom and brush our teeth. I can't help but feel just a little proud of myself for finally getting myself in here with everyone, even if it is the last day. After we shower, we get dressed and sit in the hall to wait for Ty and the morning sing.

Spike's eyes are closed, and she seems less than her usual excited self. This morning, Ty has us sing a cappella. "I know you know it by now," he says with a smile. "Let's give it up for Nina." And we sing, and there's this knocking in my chest — the reality that when I wake up tomorrow, I won't be sitting with all of these people, Ty won't be DJing my morning, Spike won't be sitting here rocking her head from side to side, smiling. Wait. Why isn't she singing?

As song ends, I elbow her in the ribs. "What's going on? Are you okay?"

"I have some bad news, Sparrow."

My heart sinks. She doesn't need to tell me the news, it's in her voice — the voice that has gone from froggy to hoarse to barely audible just in the course of the hour we've been up. It's seven thirty. The show starts at twelve. We are so, so, so completely screwed.

We go to in Heart and wait for Lara and Tanasia. They sit down with their breakfasts, waffles all around. Lara looks at hers lovingly; it'll be a long time until she sees a waffle again.

"Guys, I'm not ready to go back to food prison," she says.

"It's so unfair," says Tanasia. "I'll mail you cookies."

"We have a big problem," I say. "Has no one noticed that someone here is unusually quiet?" I gesture to Spike, who's miserably poking her oatmeal.

"I lost my voice," she mouths.

"What?" Lara looks up from her soon to be long-lost waffles.

"Spike lost her voice," I say. "What are we going to do?"

"Let's go find Ren," says Tanasia. As if she could tell we needed her, Ren is just finishing in the breakfast line.

"Go get her!" My heart is beating too fast for this early in the morning.

Ren walks over with Tanasia. She doesn't look as alarmed as she should. "Listen, guys, this is a rough break. And, Spike, I'm really sorry. I know how hard you've worked. But it happens sometimes. Particularly when you scream your face off and then sing all night long before a show." Spike blushes. "But listen, the show must go on. Figure it out, guys." She heads over to the counselors' table and digs into her waffles without a care in the world.

"Okay, what are we going to do?" asks Lara.

"We could just do the instrumentals," I say.

"I think that'll be lame," says Tanasia.

"Why don't you sing, Tanasia? You have a great voice."

"I can't. I don't know the melody well enough. I sing harmony, remember?"

"Well, I can't do it," says Lara. "I have enough on my plate just making sure my arms and legs are moving in time. I know there are people who can drum and sing at the same time, but I'm not one of them." She concocts the world's best bite of waffle (small corner, slice of strawberry, single blueberry, drizzle of syrup) and forks it. We go around and around, and don't notice that Spike has dug a pen and a pad out of nowhere and is pointing at it.

Sparrow does it, it reads.

"Like hell I do, Spike."

"Honestly, Sparrow, I don't know what else we can do," says Lara.

"Have you met me? There's no way. I'd die."

"You won't die, and we can't do it without you."

"Sparrow, the band needs you. I'm sorry. I know you don't like it, but there's nothing else to do," Tanasia says.

"There has to be something else. I can't."

"Come on, Sparrow. It's not like you don't know the damn song. After all, you wrote it."

"We all wrote it." I shoot Tanasia a look like, *What are you talking about?*

"Yeah, but only one of us wrote the first three lines. It's your song, Sparrow."

"I can't." My legs push my chair out and don't let me stop until I'm far away from Heart, from ESG, from Nina, and from the Boom Chachalacas. The bench behind Heart will be full of smoking counselors by now. I run and keep running until I find myself at Narnia.

Narnia is a weird patch of pine trees in the middle of an empty field behind the gym that we don't use. It was Lara who named it Narnia the first time we saw it. I think of the story, of the kids who disappear into a closet and find themselves in a different land. Sounds like a good deal to me. In Narnia, no one expects you to sing in front of hundreds of people like it's no big deal.

I pull up my hood and lie down on the pine needles. I'm waiting. For what? Birds? I guess. I watch them hopping from branch to branch above me, indifferent. There's not going to be any *swoop swoop* in my chest, my eyes won't grow small and round, my arms won't lift me up and out, wide and feathered. I am not about to become anything I'm not.

I watch the sky move against the branches, watch the wax-wings above me move easily from limb to limb. The world feels quiet and almost as far away as I wish it were. I stare up and up and wait. Wait to be far away from here. Wait to stop caring about what happens to the band. Wait to stop feeling my heart try to escape from my chest.

I think about Dr. K and how disappointed she'll be. She told me to enjoy this day, not to hide in the bushes. The thought of enjoying this day makes me laugh. How could anyone enjoy this? Enjoy feeling terrified? Enjoy disappointing their friends? Oh, God, and it's not just friends; Mom is on her way up here with Aunt Joan and Curtis, and it's going to be the same as always — sorry, everyone, Sparrow is too crazy to pretend to be a normal person today, show's over. Mom will worry about me, make me switch from Dr. Katz. She'll probably send me to boarding school for crazy, friendless children.

I can hear the little kids warming up. Kendra must have asked them if they're ready to rock, because even from Narnia I can hear the sound of twenty-five eight-year-olds screaming "YEAH!" The weight on my chest grows heavier. I would love to be able to get up there, to show up for the girls who have been like family to me this last month. But I don't know how. I think about Spike and how brave she is just being herself every single day, about how Lara's gentleness, which I always think will make her seem weak, only ever seems to make her stronger, and about Tanasia, who has seen me so clearly even when I wanted nothing more than to be invisible. I think about Ty coming to find me that night in the studio, how worried he was, and how relieved. I think about Nina.

Tears roll down my cheeks. I won't see these people after today. I won't have Ty telling me to open my mouth and let people know me. I won't get to see Lara take delight in all things carbohydrate. I won't get to see Spike in her boxers and undershirt, shaking her bedhead and greeting the day like a Golden Retriever. I won't get to sit in a room and play bass until my hands hurt. I don't want to leave. I don't want to miss this. I don't want to spend the last day hiding from the people who make my heart hurt with how much they give me.

With every waxwing that comes and goes overhead, I think, Dr. K, Mom, Aunt Joan, Curtis, Spike, Tanasia, Lara, Ren, Ty. They fill up the space under the trees, the space between me and the rest of the world. Maybe they're what I've been waiting for this whole time. They're not coming, though. If I want them, I'm going to need to figure out how to get up. I can hear the notes from the sound check, the little kids trying out their jams before their parents come. I think of the Boom Chachalacas, how hard it was for us to come together, how hard we've worked, how it was that we ever became friends. It doesn't seem right to screw them out of a chance to perform just because I'm more scared than I have ever been in my life. It's funny. I've woken up in a hospital with an IV coming out of my arm, but this is the scariest thing that's ever happened to me.

"Sparrow! Sparrow!" I hear Lara and Tanasia calling my name in the distance, and their voices get fainter each time. They're headed in the wrong direction. I think of how Chocolate looked for me, how good it felt to be wanted, to know that someone thought it wouldn't be the same if I wasn't there. And when I put my hand out for Chocolate's, she taught me how to fly. I keep waiting to feel ready to get up, and then it hits me—I'm not going to be ready. I'm going to have to do this without being ready.

When I come out from under the trees, the world looks the same, which surprises me. The sun should be brighter or maybe clouded over. Ty should be roaming the grounds with a concerned look on his face. Maybe a stray dog should be wandering by, or a toucan. Something to let me know that things are different than they were when I was in Narnia.

I run up to the performance tent they've set up next to ESG. Spike, Tanasia, and Lara are waiting anxiously backstage. I feel terrible for what I've put them through.

"I'm so sorry," I say, out of breath. I say it over and over, tears pouring down my cheeks.

"It's okay," says Lara. Tanasia hugs me. Spike gives me a thumbs-up.

"Listen," says Tanasia, "I didn't mean to blow up your spot like that, about your poem—"

"You've found our prodigal Sparrow!" Ty cries as he walks over. "This is a bad habit you've got, girl." He puts his hand on my shoulder.

"You're here now," says Ren, "and you guys are next."

I peek around the curtain at the sea of people. "Cool," I say, "I just have to go throw up real quick." Spike puts her hand in mine and squeezes. She shakes her head. "You'll be fine," she croaks. She passes me my makeshift tuxedo, and before I know it, Ren is passing me the bass with one hand, and pushing me onstage with the other.

"Go love them fiercely," she says, and I don't know if she's talking about the audience or the band, but before I have time to think about it, Lara's drums start, Tanasia's guitar starts, I'm playing too, but I just can't open my mouth. Lara and Tanasia aren't budging; they're just repeating the first couple of measures over and over again. I get the feeling they'll do it all day until I start singing. I see Spike in the front row. She nods at me with the beat. She smiles. She doesn't say, *Come on* or *What the hell is wrong with you?* She just smiles and nods until my mouth finds its way open. *I'm feeling restless, reckless*; it all comes easy after that. I hear Tanasia's voice mix with mine. Lara is killing it at the drums. I remember the day we all played together for the first time, the magic that lives in the four of us together. My voice isn't strong at first but it gets stronger and stronger. The beat is in my sneakers, in my hands on the strings, in my voice through the speakers. At the last chorus, the audience joins in. Their voices lift me up, my limbs go light, a familiar but totally different *swoop swoop* inside me. I've never flown this way before.

32

"Live in the flesh, Sparrow the rock star!"

It's been so long since I've been in the actual office that it seems smaller now. I sit in my seat, really her seat, and the windows seem shorter. Even Dr. K in her purple Nikes doesn't seem quite as tall.

"It's weird to be here. I can't believe I'm back."

"Do you miss camp?"

"A lot. And nothing feels normal. At home, even here. It's like nothing is different except me and now I don't feel like I fit into any of the places I fit into before."

"What does it feel like here?"

"Everything seems smaller. Like the set of an office for a TV show, not the real office. This place always felt so big to me. I remember asking you to switch seats with me way back, and now even the sky looks small."

"Follow me."

I have no idea where we're going, but I'm following her because—well, because why not? It can't be worse than sitting in the used-to-be-everything-I-needed office feeling like it can't hold me anymore.

We walk out past the lilac trim and the off-white walls, past the old *New Yorker*s and out the door. We walk down the yellow hall with the industrial carpet, that factory gray, past the shiny elevators, and through a heavy door to the stairwell. When we start walking up, I realize where we're going. I can't believe it. Seventeenth floor. This building has twenty-three. We pass eighteen, nineteen, twenty; I'm out of breath more because I'm surprised at her than because of the stairs. We pass twenty-three and come to the last step of the staircase, the one that meets with a cold metal door that says *Tenants Only*, and she takes out a key and here we are.

Arrived.

The roof.

"Really?" I ask.

"Why?" she says, smiling. "You got a thing about roofs or something?"

"I used to," I say with a laugh. "Something like that. You're not afraid I'll jump?"

"I've never been afraid of that. Are you afraid you'll jump?"

"I've only been afraid of that once."

It's beautiful. I mean, it's a Brooklyn rooftop in August. It's tar and cigarette butts and bird crap and not much else, but someone's laid down some rugs. You can sit and not feel like you're going to get stuck in the hot black tar.

"Not so small up here, is it?"

"No, this is better," I say.

"You going to fly away on me?"

"We'll see."

"Fair enough. Take a seat."

Dr. K sits cross-legged on the rug in the middle of the roof. She looks up, watching the birds come and go, maybe just watching the sky. Her hair is blowing slightly. I sit across from her like we do in the office, here in our new office with the panoramic views.

"So, what's happening at home?" she asks.

"It's okay. Mom can't believe I sang. She wants me to take voice lessons this fall."

"Do you want to?"

"Not really. But Tanasia talked about starting a band with kids at the new school. I'd like that."

"So, you guys are going to stay in touch?"

"Yeah, I mean, it's weird. It's not the same, but it's good."

"How was leaving?"

"It was hard. Spike cried a lot because she had to go back to the hellhole town she's from. She says we're the only friends she has."

"Huh, that's not what you thought when you met her."

"I guess she means close people, like people who know her real name and what a softie she is. She has to act like she's so tough at school, sometimes she doesn't remember to let it down at camp either."

I lean my head back. There's a soft, hot breeze. The kind

that doesn't make it any cooler, but it feels sweet up here. I let my head roll all the way back on my neck so all I see are clouds, birds, planes. This is what the world looked like before I jumped from the swings with Chocolate that first time. "Lara was sad because it meant the end of the frozen-yogurt vacation. Her mom came; she looks like she's made out of plastic surgery and Diet Coke. Tanasia rode back to the city with me and Mom. It was weird, like we were able to pretend that everything was fine and we were just talking like normal about music and school and whatever, and then we pulled up to her house and her parents were there and we couldn't move slow enough. We stood in the middle of the sidewalk like dumb tourists; we couldn't get out of the way. That's when we both started crying."

"Did you try to fly away?"

"From Tanasia? Absolutely not."

"Well, not too long ago crying in public would have had out you out the window."

"Yeah, but I couldn't leave her like that. I walked her to her stoop and said good-bye. It's weird, Mom being so happy to see me, and I'm just . . . I didn't really want to come home."

"Does she understand that?"

"She's going to work on it."

"And what are you working on?"

"Not lying to her about having friends, not lying to her about liking camp more than home. I mean, I'm not telling her, 'Oh, I hate it here, I like everything else more than here.'

But I told her how sad I am not to be with my friends. How it's so nice to have friends. That it's important to me that I see them again. She seems to get that. I'm hanging out with Tanasia on Friday. Mom says I can stay over there if I want. That's a big deal for her. I know it's hard for her. She's trying."

"Not a bad start."

A pigeon lands on the edge of the roof. I get quiet. I'm just watching the hazy blue and listening to traffic that seems very far away.

"It's weird being up here," I say finally, as the pigeon picks up one foot, and then the other.

"Why?"

"Because it's a roof. And not too long ago, this was the only place I ever wanted to be."

"And now?"

"I like it. I mean, I really like it. I still love seeing the birds, and I like being so far above everything. It's beautiful and calm. But it's not . . . even if I could take off right now, I wouldn't."

"Why's that?"

"I think . . ." What do I think? "I think my life is on the ground now."

"You sound surprised."

"Aren't you?"

"I always figured you'd live among us mortals eventually."

"I wasn't so sure." I stand up. I walk over to the ledge. I stand in this place where it all started. Not this roof of course,

263

but *a* roof. A snowy one, during a lunchtime winter sky break. It couldn't seem farther away from this hot tar roof and my shrink staring at my back, waiting for me to speak. I turn around and face her, smiling. This is where I want to be. Not up, not down, but right here where my feet are.

"You seem like a girl with a song in her head," she says, standing and coming toward the ledge.

"I am." What she does next surprises me, but Dr. K is full of surprises today.

"I'll take the first verse; you can take the second," she says. Then she opens her mouth and sings.

She has a nice voice, low and worn, like she smoked a lot when she was young, but full and warm, like she means every word. My arms go out wide and strong and then fall loose and easy by my sides. I take a deep breath. My chest goes open and happy.

> *I wish I could be like a bird in the sky*
> *How sweet it would be*
> *If I found I could fly*
> *I'd soar to the sun and look down at the sea*
> *And I'd sing 'cause I know*
> *How it feels to be free.*

ACKNOWLEDGMENTS

There is a long list of people without whom this book would not exist. First and foremost the amazing Arthur Levine, who has read every version of Sparrow since her wings spanned barely fifty pages, whose ability to see true north at every turn has been essential, and without whom Sparrow would sit in a drawer, shorter, sadder, and less herself. Weslie Turner, along with her extraordinary eyes and ears, has been invaluable to bringing Sparrow into the world. Her patience, vision, and insight are in every sentence of this book.

My mother, Amy Bloom, has been a tremendous guide toward not just the accurate, but toward the true in fiction, and in everything else.

Joy Marie Johannessen, not-mom and editor extraordinaire, nudged me out the gate every single time I got stuck or scared, and I got stuck and scared a lot.

Jasmine's careful eye and perfect ears make sure that Sparrow always talks like a kid and only listens to the best music. It is quite simply true in every way that there is no Sparrow without you.

Willie Mae Rock Camp for Girls and the Center for Creative Youth will recognize themselves in these pages; many thanks to both of them for letting me borrow from their schedules and their spirits.

Much love and gratitude as always to: Ms. Freyda Rose, Caitlin Moon, Alexander Moon, Donald Moon, Margret Goodwin, Kate Roberts, Ellen Shapiro, Priscilla Swan, Rae Leeper, Melissa Esmundo, Maggie Raife, Maia Cruz Palileo, Kim Katzberg, Annie, Dave and Sal Rollyson, and the wonderful Saint Ann's community.

And, of course, to the original Dr. Katz.

This book was edited by Arthur Levine and designed by Maeve Norton. The production was supervised by Rachel Gluckstern. The text was set in Baskerville with display type hand-lettered by Maeve Norton. The book was printed and bound at LSC Communications in Crawfordsville, Indiana. The manufacturing was supervised by Angelique Browne.